DEDICATION

This book is dedicated to all the people who traveled westward, carving a magnificent country out of the wilderness of America along the way. To my wife Stella who has carved a tale from my many mistakes.

Foreword

After the great Civil war many of the survivors sought a safe haven in the Promised Land called Texas. Some stayed to help a struggling republic grow into the great state it was destined to become. Some looked to steal and plunder, ever on the outside of the law, while others wanted to simply be left alone. These were the men who would seek solitude in the mountains of the west. A few stayed in Texas to trap in the Big Bend Mountain range created by a winding Rio Grande River. Others wanted to see the high country of the massive Rocky Mountain range. This is the story of one of those men.

Samson Raines would follow the wild and raging Rio Grande River from its entrance into the Big Bend canyons to its beginning somewhere in the San Juan Mountains of the Colorado territory. Along the way he would find many challenges.

ACKNOWLEDGMENTS

All scriptures and excerpts are taken from the New American Standard version of the Holy Bible. I don't think the Lord will mind.

ONE

Then we turned and set out for the wilderness by the way to the Red Sea, as the Lord spoke to me, and circled Mount Seir for day. And the Lord spoke to me, saying, You have circled this mountain long enough, Now turn north.   Deuteronomy 2: 1-3.

Samson Raines rode across a barren Texas countryside after leaving his friends along the Middle Concho River. He had lost his close friend and trapping partner to a bunch of thieves in the Chisos Mountains of Big Bend country of Southwest Texas.

Castile, a Tonkawa Indian chieftain, had left his people to go to the mountains with Samson. Now he was dead and Sam traveled the west Texas desert all alone.

Shortly after the death of his compadre, Territorial Marshall Jonah Caleb Smith had called for his help. Benjamin Stark and Abe Tobias, their warrior friends from the great civil action in the south, came along to help. The four of them had gathered to help Moses and Aaron Brown reclaim their small herd of cattle from a gang of rustlers.

Moses and Aaron Brown, with their families, had crossed into Texas with the four young fighting men. Together they had made a harrowing journey into the Promised Land called Texas. The Browns, former slaves, had found a future with a black cattle rancher called Daniel Bond.

When rustlers had stolen the herd, the Brown brothers reached out to Marshall Jonah Smith. Rancher Bond had been murdered by the rustlers, leaving the ranch to Moses and Aaron.

Sam had been happy to see that the Brown's younger brother Joshua had returned to the fold. He had been thought to be an outlaw after killing a man in San Antonio. The killing happened shortly after the Browns crossed over into Texas from a life of slavery on a Mississippi plantation. In reality Joshua had spent half his time in Texas with a Mexican family and half as a captive of Comanche Indians.

Now, as Sam rode alone he thought about the time he had spent in the mountains and looked forward to getting back to that life of solitude. He considered his options and had decided to go west until he located the Rio Grande River and follow it north to the mountains of the Colorado territory. Sam would not go back to the Big Bend. The Rio Grande was near inaccessible in the steep canyons at the bend of the river that gave the Big Bend its name. He was in no hurry to get to the river because it was now early spring and he could take his time, arriving in the high country in time to trap the northern boundaries of the great river.

Ten days on the trail brought him to Fort Stockton, an army fort occupied by union troops. While there, Sam gathered enough supplies to last until he could get to the Rio Grande. He was warned about the Apache being on the warpath where he was headed. There had been several skirmishes and the warring tribe had, on several occasions, come close enough to the fort to taunt the guards who were posted around the outer walls. They were attempting to draw the soldiers out into the open where the red men had a distinct advantage. The Calvary had pursued the Indians for months with little success. They would lure them out of the fort and then disappeared into the dry rocky terrain. On more than one occasion, they had picked off careless Calvary men, shooting them with silent missiles from the accurately short bows they were known to carry. The white men never knew from what direction an attack would come

The elusive Apache were seldom seen, nor did they leave tracks, nor signs of their whereabouts.

The mountain man had spent quite some time with the Tonkawa Indians and had heard many tales of the fierce Apache. Unlike most white men he had learned the stealth and patience of a red man. Also, unlike most white men, he wore the beaded buckskins and moccasins like an Indian.

Sam was cautious as he left Fort Stockton, keeping always on the alert for movement in the rocks. The corporal of the guard had warned him once again about them pesky redskins as the gate to the fort swung open only enough to allow him to pass through and closed quickly behind him. He did not look back as he rode slowly to the southwest.

Continuing at a walking gait he made his way to the Coyanosa Draw by late afternoon. One of the scouts of Fort Stockton had told him of a way through the arroyos to Fort Davis, between the Barrilla Mountains on the north and the Glass Mountains on the south. This would bring him to Coyanosa Draw in one day of slow riding and on to Fort Davis on the second.

"That is" he remembered the scout saying "If you keep your scalp."

Sam hobbled his horse near to the slow trickle of water in the shallow draw. There were no trees with leaves to dissipate the smoke from a fire so he was very careful to find dry mesquite sticks to build a low flame for coffee and grub. Sam constantly scanned the horizon on both sides of the draw. He knew how quietly an Apache brave could be upon him. Sam remembered his friend Jonah Smith telling him how he had been staked out by the Apache and left to die. Only the rescue by a friendly band of Tonkawa's had saved him.

The lone wolf drank hot strong coffee and ate buffalo jerky for his evening meal, snuffing out the fire as soon as the coffee pot was boiling. He settled back with his head on the edge of his saddle and a revolver in his right hand.

A night of fitful short naps finally ended and Sam built another small fire to heat the leftover coffee. He ate one of the cold biscuits, along with a strip of jerky he had acquired from Fort Stockton. As day was breaking he crossed the draw and continued on his way to the Rio Grande and up it to the mountains of the Colorado Territory.

Several times during the morning there were movements to his left and right. Sometimes he thought it might be an Apache, but never got a clean clear look. Once he saw a jack rabbit hop along unconcerned by his presence. Twice he had spotted sidewinders sliding across the hot surface of large rocks falling silently into crevices and out of sight. Sam pulled his Sharps rifle from the boot and laid it across his legs, his right index finger resting loosely on the trigger. He held the reins with a light touch in his left hand, allowing his mount to have its head. Together they moved slowly across the arid countryside.

Near noon with the hot Texas sun high in the sky Sam found an overhanging rock that provided a shade from the scorching heat.

He stepped down and gave his horse a drink, pouring water from the canteen into his cupped hand. When the horse had finished, Sam wiped his face and beard with his cool wet hand, then took a small drink himself. He removed his floppy leather hat to pour a little of the cool water over his head. Another movement caught his eye as he lifted the canteen to his lips. Again, he could not make out what it was. He pushed a cork back into the canteen and draped it over the pommel of his saddle.

Lifting the rifle he allowed it to glint in the searing sun. He wanted the Indians, if there were any, to know he was armed and ready. He chewed on another stick of jerky resting in the shade for a while, then mounted up and rode nonchalantly into the sun.

By late afternoon he came within sight of a sprawling stone walled settlement. He was nearing Fort Davis. Sam had not seen a movement in the rocks for practically an hour. If the Apache had been watching him, they chose to let him live to fight another day. He was feeling relieved and grateful as he approached the large expansive fort. His hand fell to his midsection, where he carried a copy of the New Testament Bible. He had leaned on it for four years of civil war and a year as a Texas mountain man. It made him feel close to his Maker. He whispered a silent prayer of thanks.

Sam saw a number of men armed with long guns watching as he approached the fort. He could feel many eyes following his arrival. Fort Davis was built much larger than the stockades he had seen before. In the center of a long parade ground, soldiers were marching back and forth in formation.

When he drew nearer he noticed that they were all black men. The only sound he heard was that of a sergeant calling cadence in a loud, crisp tone.

Across the way he could see four men frocked in buckskin as was he. He clucked softly and pulled the reins to turn his horse in their direction. When he reined in, one of the men acknowledged him with a simple dip of his head, another spat a long stream of brown tobacco juice onto the ground, wiping his mouth on the back of his hand.

"Howdy." The one who had spat spoke to him. "You a new scout for this buffalo soldier army?"

Sam pulled back and stepped down from his mount. "Nope…Just passing through. Stopped to see what goes on west of here… Any Injun trouble from here to the Rio Grande?" He didn't know what a buffalo soldier was, but did not let on.

"Never know. Back in sixty four a bunch of them red devils rode over to Elm Creek and killed about a dozen folks, farmers they was. Some of them that didn't get killed still live here at the fort. Hear tell they was five hunnert of them redskins rode down just lookin for whites to kill" It was the man who had tipped his head that spoke.

"Anywhere to get a hot cup of coffee?" Sam asked, not directing his question to any one of them in particular.

"Some of them farmers keeps a pot on the fire tween them buildings." The spitter told him. "I'll show you." He waved for Sam to follow, and walked with long strides across the grinder where the troops marched.

The tall mountain man followed, leading his horse behind.

"Where you headed big man?" The scout queried.

"North…. Colorado Territory."

"Lots a them red devils tween here and there. Hope you hold on to your hair."

Sam did not reply. They strode between two buildings and came upon a group of civilians gathered around a cook fire. He could smell the strong coffee brewing.

"Folks...This here mountain man needs a cup of coffee." He spat into the fire creating a steaming billow of smelly smoke. One of the women turned wearily and looked at the big man. There was a sad frightened look upon her face. She indifferently picked up an empty cup and poured it to the rim, holding it out to Sam.

"Thank you, ma'am."

"You look like you could eat a bite." She filled a blue porcelain plate with beans and dropped two biscuits alongside. Handing the plate to Sam, she ignored the other man.

The big man who liked his solitude felt uncomfortable surrounded by so many people. He quietly consumed the beans and biscuits and finished them off with a last gulp of strong coffee. The biscuits reminded him of Aaron Brown's wife, Sarah, who had fed them so well on their trek to Texas.

He thanked the group of farmers then made his way back across the grinder where three of the scouts still sat on the edge of a long porch. The soldiers were still marching up and down to the loud cadence of the burly sergeant.

"Find that coffee pot stranger?" It was the man who had tipped his head to him before.

"Yes sir...Good, hot, strong it was."

"You still planning on ridin out by yourself?" One of the others asked.

Sam put his left foot into a stirrup and swung his right leg across the saddle. "Not much for company," he answered as he swung his horse's head around and gently dug a heel into his side. He clucked and rode toward the gate. A corporal lifted the cross bar and allowed him to pass through.

"Better hang onto that hair. Them Paches sure do like scalps." Sam heard the corporal's warning as he had at Fort Stockton. There was still three hours of daylight left and he wanted to be on his way to the Rio Grande.

Luckily the young mountaineer had filled two canteens with fresh water while at Fort Davis. He had a long ride ahead of him. He traveled at a slow pace crossing over the Davis Mountains to the west of the fort. It was a hot, dry climb up the eastern slope. Down the other side would lead him into a stretch of sand desert, then another lower range of mountains before he would reach the Rio Grande. He took his time, stopping frequently to rest and cool down the animal that was his lifeline.

Always on the alert for Apaches, Sam rode until dusk and crossed over the highest peak. On the down slope he stopped in the shade of a boulder to spend the night. He did not build a fire, but chewed the buffalo jerky and drank sparingly from his canteen. He watered the horse and tethered him near a brown spot of parched grass, which was all there was for the animal.

Tomorrow Sam and his mount would tackle the twenty miles of sand. He read from his Bible in the light of the setting sun. Then he settled down for a restless night of sleep.

Winds of the Rio Grande

For, behold the wicked bend the bow. They make ready their arrows upon the string, to shoot in darkness at the upright in heart. Psalms 11:2

Three days out of Fort Davis, a dry, hot and exhausted mountain man rode onto a slightly more fertile river bank. He stopped and allowed his horse to eat the sparse bits of green and drink from the cool waters of the Rio Grande.

Sam eased into the narrow, shallow river to cool his parched body. When he was nigh on to being a redeemed man, he removed his saddle and coaxed his horse into the shallow water. Dipping the clear liquid into his floppy hat, he poured it onto the animals back. Turning to look at his master, the horse's withers trembled at the feel of the cool water. It felt good for the two of them to relax and enjoy the river.

The lone mountaineer led his horse back to the small grassy spot, and then stretched out to dry in the warm Texas sun. He nearly dozed off as he relaxed with his head on the saddle. His rifle was never far out of his reach. There was always the threat of an Apache slipping up on him. Somehow it felt good to him to be alone in Gods wilderness.

Upstream he could see a cluster of mesquite trees near the bank. When he and his horse had rested, Sam saddled his mount and led him upriver to make camp among the trees. There was more green grass for his friend at this place.

Sam built a small fire late in the afternoon. He circled stones near one of the mesquite to keep the fire from spreading. The smoke would not lift high enough to be seen by the Indians or anyone else nearby as it dissipated into the tree leaves. He made a pot of coffee and for the first time in three days enjoyed a plate of beans and biscuits to go with it.

Sam and his horse rested well in the cool Winds of the Rio Grande. At first light he rekindled the fire and had fatback to go with his biscuits and coffee. It was a wonderful world to be alone in, with only his trusty horse as a companion. He thanked the Lord for what He had given to him.

The terrain around the river was open country so Sam could see a long way in all directions. Still he carried his rifle across his legs with one finger on the trigger. Riding away from the river bank a ways, he had a better view of the flat land. He wondered what it would be like in the Colorado territory. It could not be flat and arid as was west Texas. Even in the Big Bend, trees grew tall and all around you was green. Spring flowers in the mountain country were a thing to behold.

His chain of thought was broken by a strange whooshing sound. He looked around and saw nothing. He heard the sound again and still saw nothing. Suddenly his horse stumbled and went down to his knees. He heard the whistling sound again and Sam realized what he had heard. As a second arrow went into his horses' neck, the mount toppled over, throwing Sam to the ground. Quickly he regained his wits and scrambled to the side of his horse, using him as cover from the attack. He still had seen no one and did not know in what direction the arrows had come. Think, Sam think.

His horse had been downed by two arrows on the right side of his neck, which meant in a direction away from the river. Sam quickly realized he was on the wrong side of the animal for it to afford him any protection. Another arrow hummed through the air and stuck into his saddle near his left ear. He rolled to the right to avoid another one that went into the horse's mane. He rolled over and over until he was on the opposite side, between the legs of the horse. The arrows had stopped for the moment and as Sam looked around, he knew that he had lost another friend. The animal was dead.

Slowly Sam raised his head to peer back across the saddle, removing the canteens from the pommel. He saw nothing, heard nothing. Were they still out there? With his head down he looked over his shoulder toward the river. He saw nothing. Where had they gone? He wondered. The sun had gone into the middle of the sky and still he heard nothing. He took a small drink of water, from one of the canteens. What was next? His horse was dead and he was a lone man in a wild country. It was their country. Would they kill him where he lay? Sam began to pray, not for his rescue, but for whatever God's will was for him. He was ready to die if that be the Lord's will, although he would love to see the mountains first.

It seemed like forever, but the sun finally crossed into the west, creating a huge orange and grey sky. Sam had not seen nor heard a sound since that last arrow had finished off his mount. He was still gathering his wits about him. When the sun was over the horizon he made a decision to try to make it to the river. He removed what little jerky he had left and a box of cartridges from his saddle bag. Scooting backward on his belly he moved a couple of feet then stopped to listen. He kept up the slow crawl, stopping frequently to look and listen. After two hours he felt his feet drop into the waters of the river. He slid back until he was waist deep. His feet were on the muddy bottom. He crouched down and gradually made his way along the river bank to the north. The Lord had saved him for now and he was still planning on making the Colorado territory.

Why did the Apaches not pursue him? Did they leave him to the elements? He crept silently along, being careful not to splash the water. He was sure the Indians were close enough to hear any sound he made.

He had heard about the Apache from his friend Castile of the Tonkawa tribe. They would hunt you for days, always out of sight but ever looming. They were a heartless people when it came to white men, and fierce warriors among the other tribes. Sam knew he was at their mercy. He also knew they had no mercy. They would track a man for days just to watch him die.

With these thoughts in mind Sam made a decision to travel only at night and seek a hiding place in the daytime. He would have to stay within reach of the river for water to sustain him. He remembered again the story told to him by Marshall Jonah Smith about being staked out by these savages.

All night long he moved slowly along the river bank, sometimes in the water and sometime on the rocks when the water was too shallow. Sam calculated he had gone about two miles when the sky was beginning to turn light in the eastern sky over the Davis Mountains. He crawled away from the river and found shelter enough to hide himself from the hot sun and maybe the Apache.

He thought of the morning before when he had had a pot of coffee to warm him and food to eat. The jerky would not last long and he would have to start thinking about finding food. There was food to be had but getting to it while the Apache watched him would be tough to do. He slept off and on during the day, listening each time he woke for any sound of his pursuers.

At the first sign of the sun setting in the west, he considered his predicament. He did not want to spend another night in the cold waters of the river. This night he would remain upright like a man and try to put more distance between him and the red devils that followed him.

He stumbled along feeling every rock through his thin, worn moccasins. It was hard to make time in the dark, especially trying to move quietly. After about two hours he stepped out of the rocks and onto a sandy strip of ground. It felt so much better on his feet that he didn't care if he left tracks. The Indians probably knew where he was anyway. Just before day he was back walking in the small stones again.

Sam began to cast an eye across the horizon for boulders large enough to conceal a man. There were two pretty big ones with another straddling across the top of them, creating a small crevice barely large enough for the big man to crawl into. He slid into the opening feet first so he could still see the surrounding terrain. Lying on his belly Sam ate the last of the jerky, then laid his head on one arm and went to sleep. As the day before he was constantly awakening to listen for the sounds of his enemy.

The western sun was on his face when he woke, with a growling in his belly. He was hungry.

As he began to crawl from his hiding place, he heard a now familiar sound. It was the sound of an arrow cutting through the crisp evening air. The arrow hit the upper boulder and fell to the ground in front of him. Sam pushed himself back into the crevice and held his rifle at the ready. He lay that way until the sun was below the western mountains of Mexico. They were playing with him, letting him know they were still with him.

Crawling again out of the rock opening, Sam twisted and move his body in all directions, trying to relieve the stiffness in his bones. How long would they track him? How long could he survive in this situation?

He began once more, a slow painful walk northward along the Rio Grande. His feet were beginning to blister as his moccasins wore through on the somewhat sharp river rocks.

Sometime in the night Sam saw the red eyes of a rabbit in the moonlight, but could not risk a shot. Then he noticed he was near a clump of mesquite. He cut a long slim limb and stripped it to bare wood, to make it limber. Another trick his friend Castile had given him.

All the time he had watched the eyes of the furry creature who had not yet seen him. Cautiously he crept along, keeping the animal's eyes in the moonlight, but not so it could detect his approach. Sneaking ever so slowly Sam was close enough to swing the limber stick in an arc, striking the rabbit in a downward motion just behind the ears. It quickly went down, impulsively kicking both front and rear feet, expiring from a broken neck. The hungry man in very short order gutted and skinned the dead animal.

In one swift move Sam had found food and a furry animal skin to wrap around his feet. Not wanting to arouse his followers, he ate the hindquarters of the rabbit raw. He would save the skin till he was again resting in the daylight, and then make a set of moccasins. Despite his sore and bleeding feet Sam thought he had made more time on his third night, partly because there was more sand than rock, and partly because the food had helped his outlook. He would hang onto the front half of the animal carcass till daylight even though the smell was awful.

His routine continued. He searched out shelter for another day. Sam knew by the arrow the day before, that he wasn't hiding from his enemy, only prolonging his life in the crevices of rocks. This morning he would build a fire with his flint stone and knife. He would, if God wanted, die on a full stomach of cooked rabbit. He savored every bite and chewed every bit of meat from the bones. His attitude adjusted somewhat by a hot meal, Sam first wrapped his feet in rabbit skin moccasins he had made, then elevated them on a rock and went to sleep. Again he kept waking and listening for the sound of approaching footsteps, though he was sure he would not hear them if they came.

At dusk, once again, he heard the familiar sound of an arrow and watched it fall to the ground. This time he picked it up and stuck it behind his back in his belt. "May come in handy." Sam was startled to hear his own words spoken aloud. He looked around to see if anyone else had heard. "Must be losing it?" He spoke again out loud. He shook his head and began to once again follow the river north. Sometime in the night the mountain man crossed over the river and turned his journey to the west. He was headed for the high country.

The Apache, too, were at home in the higher elevation, but Sam felt he had followed the river long enough to maybe throw them off his trail. He had been very careful going in and out of the water, so the red men might not find where he had gone.

By day break he was in the foothills and shelter for his days was becoming more abundant. He found a small overhanging cliff that would provide him with shade and a good view of the Rio Grande. His sleep was more peaceful and he slept in longer sessions, although when he did wake he listened intently for any sound.

About midday he was suddenly awakened by a faint rustling noise. He lay very still with his eyes closed, trying to discern the sound. Opening one eye slowly he looked around his hideaway. The sound had seemed very close to him. A sage brush began to wave, but the wind was not blowing hard enough to cause it to sway. Concentrating on the brush for some time, Sam saw a movement he had seen before. A sidewinder unaware of his presence came slithering into his shady shelter. Easing his knife from the sheath, he calmly drove the tip of the blade into the back of the reptile's head. A reflex action sent the long tail up the knife and it wrapped around the trapper's arm. Sam pushed harder on the blade until the snake relaxed its coil from around his arm. He skinned the fresh kill and threw the head and skin into the brush for some animal to have. He didn't have time to clean and dry the skin for his own use.

There was a small cave like opening in the rear of his shelter, no bigger than a small animal. Sam gathered some dry sagebrush and small limbs from mesquite that lay scattered on the ground. Most of the smoke, what little there was, would not show from any distance. He punctured the snake in several places and threaded it onto a long mesquite stick and roasted it over the small fire. In a short time he had devoured the entire thing.

He went back to sleep and woke when the sun was gone from view. There had been no arrow fired at him this day. He felt somewhat safer as he resumed his journey. It was a starry moonlit night, which made it easier to maneuver in the rocky foothills, and easier to navigate by the North Star.
Sam stuck to the hills throughout the night and had made good time by daylight.

Smoke…Just as day was breaking he smelled smoke. It stopped him in his tracks. Where? Another odor infiltrated his nostrils. It was an odor he longed for. It was the smell of boiling coffee. He stopped and scanned the horizon in all directions.

Whoever it was knew how to build a fire. Do Apaches drink coffee? The Indians he had met did not like the dark brew. It must be white men. He caught a small wisp of smoke coming from behind an outcropping to the west. Stealthy Sam made his way toward the smoke and smell of coffee. He climbed up on a large boulder that should give him a line of sight to the fire. As he peeked over the edge he saw two men seated on the ground next to the fire. They both wore large sombreros. Both were eating rolled flour tortillas with refried beans inside. The roasted sidewinder had long been gone from his belly.

One of the two Mexicans got to his feet and walked slowly to where two burros were tied to a mesquite tree. Sam was concentrating on the food and coffee when he heard a loud voice.

"Come down gringo… or I shoot you in the head." The man at the burros pointed a rifle at him. Sam raised both hands, then turned and slid feet first from his perch. He thought he had been unseen.

"Drop the gun senor." The one holding the rifle spoke again. Sam lowered his right arm and bending, dropped his rifle gently onto the ground.

"What you want Gringo?" The same man spoke again, while the other one picked up Sam's rifle from where he had dropped it.

"Food"… Sam pointed to the fire "Coffee"

"Paches… they kill you cayuse," we see. "Why you no dead?"

"Lucky, I guess. Can I have a cup of that coffee?"

"Si senor, I am Rapheal. That one Pedro. He no speak gringo."

"I am Samson Raines…. You can call me Sam."

"What you do out here all alone? You crazy?"

"Maybe so…. I am going to the Colorado Territory….When I get a cayuse." Sam used the Mexican word for horse.

"You no make it senor….The Paches will kill you. They play with you, but not for long."

"How do they not kill you?" Sam was curious. They had watched the Apaches shoot his horse, but they seem to ride free on their burros.

"They no see us….They kill us too. Paches no like Mexicans. Aficionados put …how you say…bounty on Pache scalps. Fifty pesos for man, twenty five on squaw, ten pesos on ninas e ninos. Paches no like." Raphael looked very serious.

"How do you stay out of their way?"

"We no stay long one place. Like you we move. Pache no go too far in Mexico…. Lose scalp." He motioned across his head as if to take his own scalp. "You stay today…, Sleep tonight….Then you go. Eat beans now… Drink café."

Sam stayed and visited with the Mexicans. He learned that the Indians were Lupan Apache. Their war chief is Victorio. He is a mighty war chief for the Lupan and Mescalero. The great warrior had fought the white man with Cochise and Geronimo. He was with the small band of braves that toyed with him.

Now, at least Sam knew who his enemy was. He would stay with the Mexicans till dawn and be on his way again. This time he would travel in the daytime. The Apache seemed to always know where he was anyway.

As soon as it was sundown, the two Mexican wrapped themselves in serapes and went to sleep. Sam moved away from the camp and found as before a crevice to sleep in.

At dawn Sam woke to an eerie quiet. He crawled out of his stone bed and looked to the Mexicans camp. Both of them were still wrapped in serapes. When he looked around the area, he felt something was wrong.

Suddenly he saw that the two burros were no longer tied to the mesquite tree. He cautiously approached the fire ring from the day before. The ashes were cold. In the center of the gray pile of ash there was one stark difference. A lance was standing alone vigil over the camp. Sam's heart began to race as he realized he was in a vulnerable position out in the open. Had the Mexicans not heard the intruders?

He slowly crept to where the two were sleeping. When he drew close he found they were not sleeping. Blood was still oozing out of a gaping hole at their necks. The sombreros were covered with blood.

Sam did not have to remove them to know what was underneath. The two Mexican men, who had welcomed him into their camp the day before, had lost their scalps and their lives.

There was not time to hang around to bury them. Sam closed his eyes for a moment and asked the Lord for mercy on their souls, then ducked into the rocks and again began his journey to the north.

THREE

Now, my father, see! Indeed, see the edge of your robe in my hand! For in that I cut off the edge of your robe and did not kill you, know and perceive that there is no evil or rebellion in my hands, and I have not sinned against you, though you are lying in wait for my life to take it 1Samuel 24;11

Moving quickly through the rocks, Sam wanted to distance himself from the ruthless killing of the two men. They were slaughtered because they had befriended him. A sick feeling came over him, recalling the blood soaked faces of two of God's creations.

He didn't have time to think about those things. Sam knew he had to keep his wits about him if he wanted to get away from the murderous savages who were pursuing him. On sore painful feet he quickened his pace. Were they waiting for him? After an hour of fast moving he stopped and leaned against a large boulder to catch his breath. He felt the heat that the rock had absorbed from the sun's rays. His feet were throbbing and he knew he could not keep up this speed for very long.

As he gathered his thoughts, his mind went back to a time in the Deep South. A desperate confederate army was in defeat and on the run. It was the last time Samson Raines had retreated from anything or anyone. He made up his mind right then. If he retreated, those red savages, led by a warrior chief, would hunt him down and kill him, the same way they had done the two Mexicans.

It was time to go from pursued to pursuer. What would be the first priority? Weapons! He carried a Sharps rifle and a revolver left over from the civil conflict. In his possibles pouch he had a box of cartridges. He would only use firearms when the situation dictated. Giving away his position was something he did not dare to do. He also had a knife in his belt sheath. That would be the weapon of choice for now. He must remain as silent as possible. He remembered, as a much younger warrior, the tactic of hit and run employed by confederate forces. It worked then and it would have to work now. The arrow? He had stuck it in his back waist band. Sam would return it to its owner.

First of all he must make a bow to shoot the arrow with. He should have retrieved the other arrows the

Apache had shot at him. His mind was racing. Slow down Sam!

This time when he began the trip north, it would be with a different purpose. This time he would not seek a hiding place. His shelter now must be a war room. In order to survive this ordeal, he must plan every move.

First, he must find the right material for a bow. There were plenty of mesquite trees around. What about a string to propel the arrow? He would have to find long straight shafts to make more arrows with.

Sam kept on the move, constantly being aware of his surroundings. He had been careless before, leaving tracks for the savages to follow. Not now. He was searching ahead finding places to put his feet before he took a step.

He knew the Apache was a cunning hunter. They were never seen, but then he had never really looked for them. He had only run from one hiding place to another.

Stopping to rest in a cluster of mesquite trees, Sam found the limb he was searching for. He didn't need a very long one, just long enough to propel an arrow, but short enough to be able to maneuver in tight places. The rest of that day he used it for a walking stick, to help him hobble along.

Before dusk, he found a place to spend another night away from the trackers. This time he approached a crevice, leaving sign for them to follow. He then backtracked in his own footprints and found another location close by to rest.

He spent the remaining day light working on the shaft he had chosen for a bow. First, he removed all the bark and scraped until he had a smooth surface. Using his sharp knife, he cut a notch at each end to hold a string in place. Finally, he removed his buckskin trousers and untied the short rawhide strips that held each of the legs together on the outside. With his knife he cut a long strip from bottom to top. He re-tied the trouser leg together and put his pants back on. He pulled and stretched the long strip to make sure it was strong enough to work. He tied the rawhide strip to one end of the bow in the notch he had carved. Shoving that end into a small crevice, he bent the bow into a curve and tied the other end of the string in place. He loaded the one Apache arrow into the bow and tested the draw. He was satisfied that it would serve his purpose,

Sam slept well that night, proud to be back in control of his life. He thanked the Lord for bringing him to this point.

After a good night's rest, he looked around carefully, and then left the shelter. He made his way to a place where he could see the fake shelter he had created. There was another Apache arrow on the ground near it. Sam smiled for the first time in a long while.

He moved out and traveled cautiously, always to the north. At midday a cluster of prickly pear cactus appeared before him. The pears were abundant and Sam harvested six of them, being careful not to touch them with his bare hands. He cut them free from the Nopal pad, allowing them to fall to the ground. He then rolled them onto a flat rock with his new bow. Being careful not to touch the spiny fruit, he cut the thicker top and bottom off, and sliced them the long way just through the skin. Utilizing the slit he peeled the skin away with his fingers, using his knife to hold them in place. He ate the purple pulpy fruit, spitting the hard seeds onto the ground.

After filling himself with the tasty cactus fruit Sam found a spot nearby in the rocks. Looking all around, he sat back and waited. An hour later, two redskin men suddenly appeared on his back trail. He watched as they found his eating place. They bent down to take a closer look at his leftovers, pointing and arguing. One of the two spoke very loudly, raised his arms and stood erect. Sam let fly an arrow and caught him squarely in the chest. He bellowed and pitched forward into the cactus bed. The other one disappeared rapidly into the rocks. One down, Sam was pleased with his action. The battle was on.

He stayed put and kept his eyes on the spot where the other Apache had gone. Seeing no movement, he backed away until he had put some distance between himself and the cactus forest. Then he quietly and swiftly made his way to the river bank. He settled into a cropping of sagebrush and lying prone, waited and watched the river.

He was no longer in a hurry to get to the Colorado territory. He just wanted to stay alive.

When the sun had gone down at his back, he slowly crawled the few feet to the river and slid quietly into the cold water. The water was shallow enough to wade through at this point and Sam took his time crossing to the other side. When he reached the other bank When he reached the other bank, he got down and crawled until he had moved fifty yards away from the river and into the rocks. He was back in Texas.

He stayed on the move being ever watchful of his surroundings. He had heard that Indians didn't attack at night and he thought about the encampment where two Mexicans had lost their lives. He traveled to what he figured was near midnight and found a place where he could see his back trail and be out of sight. He slept till dawn.

One of his priorities today must be food. Since he had left the dead Mexicans he had only eaten prickly pears. If he was to stay in the battle with the Apache he would have to keep his strength. He could use another animal skin to replace his worn rabbit skin moccasins.

There was that sound again, the sound of an arrow singing through the early morning air. He looked up just in time to see an arrow coming straight at him. His reflex moved him to the right enough to catch the arrow in the fleshy part of his upper left arm. Through the pain he lifted his rifle with his right arm and fired at an Apache on a boulder twenty yards away and above him. The Indian let out a shriek and toppled headlong from the boulder. Sam saw two others circling his position, one on the left and one on the right. He got off a shot to the one on the left that missed and ricocheted off a rock. Quickly swinging the Sharps around, he pulled the bolt back and forced another brass into the chamber. He managed to fire and hit the other one, killing him with a bullet to the head.

Sam did not know how many others there were, but he knew he could not remain where he was. His left arm was bleeding and painful, but he had time only to break the arrow off enough to prevent it from catching on the underbrush. He moved through the rocks looking in all directions before he advanced. Sam had gotten two more of his enemy. He knew there was at least one more out there.

The injured mountain man stumbled along, feeling the head of the arrow in his arm. He felt over his shoulder and found it had penetrated through the skin on the back side of his arm. It had to come out.

Finding a flat place on one of the boulders, Sam leaned against it with the three inch long broken stub in contact with the hard surface. He removed his floppy hat and stuffed it into his mouth to choke off the screams. He took a deep breath and pushed his left arm hard against the rock. The severe pain put him to his knees. Perspiration flowed freely down his back along with blood from the open wound.

Reaching again over his shoulder, with his right hand he extracted the broken arrow. Thankful that the hat in his mouth had silenced his scream, he fell to the ground and sat until the pain diminished. When he was again able to get to his feet, he checked the terrain around him once again.

Slowly he staggered his way to the river and fell to a prone position. He crawled far enough in to allow the cold water to flow over and through the throbbing hole in his arm. It burned at first, but then the cold water numbed the pain to a tolerable level and slowed the bleeding. Sam knew that he must find a place to hide and tend to the wound. He got to his feet and continued up the river. The pain in his arm and the hunger in his belly, were bringing him to near delirium. Where were the Apache? He was finding it hard to concentrate. He didn't know how long he had stumbled along, but the terrain was changing from a flat desert to higher elevation hills. It was becoming more difficult to navigate. He staggered through the rocks, not knowing which hurt the most, his arm or his feet. Both were hurting badly. Sam was beginning to need to maintain his balance by leaning into boulders. The moving was slow. Sam, not thinking, leaned on his left shoulder and the excruciating pain made him recoil. He fell hard to the right. There was no boulder to catch him and he felt himself falling.

Suddenly the gray light of a setting day turned to a pitch black night. He felt as if he was falling into a never ending well spinning and tumbling He fell, feverishly unconscious.

When Sam opened his eyes, he still could not see. He did not know where he was or how long he had been there. He groped around and found his Sharps there, lying right next to him. He lay very still in the darkness trying to get his bearings.

Where was he? Was he dead? Was this hades?

He felt something under his head and reached up to touch it. It was one of his canteens. The pain in his arm had subsided somewhat. When he touched it he found it was covered with some kind of crude bandage.

His eyes were beginning to adjust to the dark and he felt a cool dampness in the air around him. The more his vision cleared, the better he could see. He determined he was in some sort of huge cavern. Across the way, he saw remnants of what had been a fire. There were bones scattered about. Someone had eaten many meals in here. He smelled something familiar to him and it smelled like food... like jerky. It had that salty beefy odor. Lying next to his canteen on a straw mat was a stack of what appeared to be buffalo jerky. Who did this? Who fixed my shoulder? He picked up a piece of jerky and took a bite. It was so good. The starving man ravenously ate all the jerky and felt around for more. He took a long drink of water from his canteen then settled back.

How long had he been there? Sam had no idea how much time had passed since his fall. Time enough for his wound to partially heal. Time enough for someone to bandage it.

He got to his knees and began to move around. He could see a faint glow of light coming in from some kind of opening. He inched his way cautiously toward it. Outside the dark room that he was in was another larger room. This one had an opening to the outside. He started to get to his feet when suddenly a shadow blocked out the light. He stopped and backed quickly into the darkness.

A figure entered the cave and Sam recognized him as an Apache Indian. The tall red man walked slowly toward the injured man, not knowing he was there. Sam's eyes had adjusted to the dark, but the Indians had not. The red man walked to within five feet of him, turned and squatted on his haunches. He made a grunting sound and began to relieve himself. Sam could have reached out and touched him. He didn't

He saw a bone handled knife protruding from the Apache's waistband. The mountain man deftly removed the knife and waited motionless for the Indian to miss it. Just as Sam decided to put the blade into his enemies back, the Indian rose and tramped proudly toward the opening and out of the cave.

The mountaineer picked up his rifle and followed. When he stepped out into the light he saw two Indians with their backs to him. He raised his rifle to fire, but something made him hesitate. He lowered his weapon and spoke loudly, "Victorio!"

Sam held the knife he had removed from one of them high above his head with his sore arm. He was guessing one of them was the Apache chief.

Both of them wheeled to face him. One reached down and touched his empty knife sheath: the other raised a bow. The one with no knife raised his hand to stop the other from shooting.

"I, Victorio!" He stopped and stared at Sam standing motionless. He reached with both hands and removed a medallion from around his neck and laid it on the ground at his feet.

"I am Apache Wolf... You go in peace." He turned and walked away, head held high.

When they were out of sight Sam retrieved the medallion made of wolf's teeth. It reminded him of his friend Castile, also a man of the wolf.

FOUR

> Then David said to the Philistine, "You come to me with a sword, a spear, and a javelin, but I come to you in the name of the Lord of hosts, the God of the armies of Israel whom you have taunted.
> 1 Samuel 17:45

The Apache party had disappeared completely. They were no longer a threat to Sam. He decided to remain around the cave until his wound had healed. Now he could hunt the surrounding country with no fear of attack by the Apache. Still, he used the bow to diminish his chance of being spotted.

The cave was located near the river, so Sam could sit outside and observe anyone traversing it without being seen. He spent his days scouting the immediate area, seeking food and at other times just observing what was around.

On several occasions, Sam felt as though he were being watched. He had nothing to go on, just a premonition that someone was always near. Maybe the Apache were still watching him!

---------- ….. ----------

One week after the encounter with Victorio, Sam walked out of the cave after a peaceful night's sleep. To his surprise, sitting on a rock near the cave entrance was a coffee pot. He recognized it straightaway as his own. Alongside the pot was a canvas bag with coffee and another with flour. All of these things had been left on his dead horse. How did it get here? Sam scanned the river and all around and saw nothing. He saw no one and no movement. He started a fire from mesquite twigs which were in abundance on the ground. When the fire was burning, he walked to the river and filled the pot with water. It would be so good to enjoy a cup of coffee again. He had not even thought of a cup to drink from until he opened the aromatic bag of dark grounds, and found inside was his own cup. Again he looked around for his visitor.

A new attitude and fresh coffee every morning made his healing go much faster.

Sam began to dig into his mind about recent events. He had nearly lost his life more than once in the last month. Falling into the cave had been a God- thing. Nothing else could explain it. The Apache chieftain sparing him had been a God - thing. Had God put the canteen beneath his head? Had God put a crude bandage with some sort of healing poultice on his wound? No matter who had actually performed the aid, it was a God - thing.

After another week of hanging around the cave and recuperating, Sam was ready to continue his journey up the Rio Grande.

When he awoke, and while his eyes were still accustomed to the dark, he gathered his rifle, canteen, and possibles pouch then stepped out into a new day, He would have coffee before he began the long walk.

As he poured the last of the coffee into a cup, the sound of rustling brush caught his ear. He tensed and listened intently. There was another noise Sam had heard before. It was the sound of a snorting horse. It was a very distinct sound. He listened to see if he were hearing things. Where would a horse come from? Where is the rider? He heard the snort again and lifted the Sharps to be ready. Nothing moved. He crept in the direction of the nicker. Pushing aside the brush with the rifle barrel, Sam saw a paint Indian pony. It was tied to a mesquite tree. He froze in his tracks, looking and listening. When he had looked all around, his eyes came back to the animal. The horse had turned his head and was staring directly at him. On the ground near the horse's side was a brand new pair of moccasins. They were an exact copy of the ones he had disposed of somewhere along the trail. Did the Apache leave them?

Cautiously Sam approached the animal. He squatted and picked up the moccasins with one hand, while holding the Sharps tightly in the other. Checking all around once more he untied the horse with the hand holding the moccasins. Very slowly he backed out of the brush and turned toward the cave. There was no one around, anywhere!

Back by the mouth of his hiding place, Sam began to prepare to leave. He was ready to leave from the dark cavern that had been his refuge while his wound healed.

Sam managed to get his cup and coffee pot into the canvas bag, since his coffee supply was getting so low. He removed the rawhide thong from the bow and tied the flour and coffee bags together.

The paint pony looked at him curiously as he draped the booty across his back. Sam was going to miss the bow. It had provided him with many meals and had allowed him to dispose of more than one of the Apache.

One last look and Sam swung himself onto the back of his new mount. It felt good to be on horseback again.

He had discarded the rabbit skin foot covering for the new pair of moccasins. They were identical to his other pair, right down to the beading. His feet were practically back to normal. A few days on horseback would make them feel even better.

A pang of remorse came over him as he rode the pony up along the river bank. For the first time in a year, he felt lonesome. He had been a loner ever since he came to Texas. The only human he had spent time with was his friend Castile. He was beginning to miss the companionship they had shared.

Sam shook the feeling off and tried to concentrate on the trail before him. The terrain was starting to change again. He had come through an area of low mountains and now it was flattening again. He kept a wary eye on his surroundings.

His enemy Victorio had told him to go in peace. Did the other Apache know? Sam fingered the wolf teeth medallion hanging about his neck. He slid his hand down and felt for the New Testament in his waist band. He put his faith in the Bible. The red men put theirs in things like the teeth around his neck.

The mountain man rode slowly through the day. Sam kept a sharp lookout while still trying to keep his mind on the journey. Several times he thought he had seen some fleeting movement across the river, though unable to get a clear view. He could not determine if he had been seeing things.

Sam pulled on the makeshift halter around the horses head. He sat and scanned the area, looking for a place with some cover to spend the night. Ahead on the edge of the river bank was a cluster of mesquite trees. He approached guardedly and concluded that it was a safe place.

He stepped down and allowed the pony to drink from the clear, cold river. Once again in the arid Texas land, Sam gathered mesquite branches from the ground, building a small fire to make a pot of coffee. While the water boiled, he found some prickly pears and again went through the procedure for removing the inner pulp. This time he threaded it onto a stick and heated it over the low flame. It was another way to prepare food from the land. Castile had passed the knowledge on to him. How many times would Castile save him?

Sam had mixed river water with some of his flour. Toasted over the fire it would make a tortilla to wrap the fruit in. He was satisfied with a full belly again and enjoyed the last cup of coffee as the sun was setting over a Mexico horizon.

In the early morning light Sam put his last pot of coffee on the fire. He had filled the pot and canteen from the river. He thought he had heard a rustling sound again and after looking up and down the bank, had brought the pot to the fire. He scanned the horizon once more. His eyes fell on somethin something at the base of one of the trees. It was a bamboo mat stacked with jerky. It was just like the time at the cave. He looked around again then he ate a breakfast of jerky and hot coffee.

Back on the horse, he continued to look around for his benefactor. He saw no one. Sam clucked his horse's head around and started another long day on the move. It was late spring now and he had lost a month of travel time. He had hoped to reach the headwaters of the Rio Grande before the first snow covered the landscape.

The thundering of hooves abruptly disturbed his thought. He turned and saw a small party of Apache closing in on him from the rear. They swiftly came alongside him, six on each side. Yelping and raising weapons above their heads they taunted him. Sam sat very still on his horse and watched as the raucous Indians circled around him. He was at their mercy. He felt sure that if he raised his rifle he would be killed.

He remembered hearing from his Tonkawa friends about red men making a coup. It meant touching an enemy without killing him, then riding away to taunt them. Sam had never heard about Apache taking coup. They were a murderous warring tribe set on destroying their enemy.

They continued riding away and back in groups. They jabbed at him constantly with lances. Sam felt the pain as one of them tapped his left shoulder. His expression did not change. Another of them poked at his chest lifting the wolf teeth medallion until it came out from inside his buckskin shirt. When the Apache spotted the necklace around Sam's neck he stopped jabbing and began speaking to the others in the Apache tongue. It caused them to stop what they were doing. When all of them had seen Victorio's medallion, they rode away in silence. It was over as quickly as it had begun.

Sam touched the medallion and thanked the Lord that Victorio had given it to him. It would be his passage through Apache territory. He left it hanging on the outside of his shirt. A spiritual calm surrounded him as he rode on to continue his quest.

The rest of the day was uneventful and Sam began to enjoy the quiet beauty of the Rio Grande River. Several times he saw movement on the Mexican side of the river. Once he spotted two burros in the low hills. He wondered if it were the two he had seen in a camp days before. They quickly disappeared into the rocks and Sam rode on.

Who had left the jerky? He was confident it was not the Apache.

He bedded down that night amongst the rocks. The mesquite trees were becoming sparse now. He made no fire because his coffee supply was depleted. He munched on the last strip of jerky he had saved from the morning.

He could see a mountain range off to the northwest. The sun went down over the south slope. It didn't look as tall as the Chisos in the Big Bend Mountains. He wondered what they were.

Sam had to eat cactus pears and tortillas for breakfast again. He yearned for a hot cup of strong coffee to go along with them.

The sun was still low in the eastern horizon as he mounted the pinto and followed the river. It seemed to be headed right into the mountains.

Sam saw someone walking along the river bank in the distance. It was a man leading a burro. When he got close enough, Sam could see he was a stoop shouldered old man with a white beard and wearing a sombrero.

"Howdy stranger," the dark skinned old man spoke.

"Howdy," Sam replied. He was surprised to hear English from a man he thought to be Mexican.

"Headed to El Paso are ye?"

"Headed where this river takes me," Sam answered.

"Seen any of them Paches out yonder?" The old man pointed over Sam's shoulder.

"A few," He felt a twinge in his left shoulder.

"Still got your scalp? You be one of the lucky ones. Paches don't cater to whites much." He looked at Sam with a curious awe.

"They tried." Sam returned. "They don't bother you?"

"Not me." He reached into his shirt. "Got me one of them things too." Out of his shirt he pulled a medallion similar to the one Sam wore around his neck "See any gold out there?"

"Weren't looking for any. Good luck old timer." Sam spurred the pinto and rode past the old man.

Sam had heard of El Paso from the Tonkawa. It was the last place before leaving Tejas. Not knowing what lay ahead, he was still relieved that he would be leaving the Apache territory.

FIVE

"So do not worry about tomorrow; for tomorrow will care for itself. Each day had enough trouble of its own.   Matthew 6:34

Sam rode into the south side of El Paso, Texas. It was a busy teeming town of two thousand people. The last time he had seen so many was on a battle ground at Vicksburg, Mississippi.

There was a mixture of cultures in this town. El Paso is located on the border of Mexico. Most of the people who resided in the town were from south of the border. Some others wore braids down their backs and funny little caps and their eyes were slanted.

There were whites who had come to escape the results of a long civil war. A small number were true Texans, bent on creating a lawful state out of a rugged republic. Some were passing through on their way to a wide open frontier.

Sam Raines fit into the latter. He felt very uncomfortable with all the commotion of town living. He would find what few supplies he needed and follow the river back out of this hubbub.

He passed saloons with drunken cowboys staggering in and out of swinging doors. There were the pigtails scurrying along with baskets full of laundry, Mexicans were everywhere. Some of them were sweeping sand from the board walk while others were taking a siesta where ever they found a place to sit or lay.

A sign over one of the doors read Montoya Mercancias Generales. In his limited Spanish, Sam translated that to mean Montoya General Store.

He slid off the pinto and tied him to the hitching rail in front of the establishment. Stepping over a sleeping Mexican he walked through double screen doors into the store building. It was much larger on the inside than he expected. It truly was a general merchandise store. There was a little of everything.

He spotted a section in the back with food items. Some were in cans and box containers on the shelves. Others, such as pickles, crackers, flour, and coffee, were in large barrels with lids. The name of each product was written on the sides of the barrels. He saw what read Café and figured it was coffee. He had heard that word from a Mexican man who had offered him hospitality.

Sam looked around and found himself to be the only gringo in the store. A short graying man with a mustache came up behind him. He smiled, "Pueda le ayuda, Senor?"

The tall, bearded mountain man felt out of place and shrugged at the shorter man.

"Ah… You no comprendo. May I help you senor?" He smiled again.

"Coffee… Café." Sam stammered.

"Ah… Si Senor." He stepped to the barrel and retrieved a scoop hanging alongside the large container.

Sam handed him the leather bag containing his pot, cup and the smell of coffee.

The Mexican storekeeper removed the cup and coffee pot and put them into a new clean leather bag. He filled Sam's bag with a fresh aromatic blend of coffee.

"Gracias Senior." He handed Sam the full bag.

Sam held out his hands. One contained loose change and the other one a can of peaches. The store keeper took the amount he wanted and said, "Gracious."

Sam stepped out onto the boardwalk with his two leather bags glad to be away from all the chatter inside.

When he looked up, two scroungy looking white men were checking out his animal.

"You live with them red devils?" One of them snarled through tobacco stained teeth.

Sam answered, "No, just riding one of their horses."

"Wouldn't buy from no Mex." The other one spat into the street. They were looking for a fight.

Sam slipped the thong from over the hammer of his six gun. He was holding the coffee bag low enough to hide his right hand, so neither of them saw the action. He noted that neither of them had done the same.

"What's that there necklace you got on? Looks like a redskin necklace to me." The first man snarled again.

The sleeping Mexican rolled over and scampered away on his knees. The others, who were near, scrambled away too.

"Just move away from my horse and I'll be on my way"

The two men, spoiling for a fight, backed out into the street side by side.

"What are you? Mex or Apache!"

Sam stepped down the step and went around to the off side of the pinto. Using his left hand, he slung the bags over his horse's back, keeping his right hand near his revolver.

"What you wearin them moccasins fer?" "Yore squaw chew that hide ?"

One of the two men released the hammer thong and reached for his revolver. He only got it half way clear of his holster when a bullet from Sam's six gun slammed into his heart. The man's eyes had a shocked look as he fell onto his back into the dusty street.

The other man stumbled and backed away. There was a look of fear in his protruding eyes. He swallowed the wad of tobacco in his mouth. "Don't shoot mister." He turned and ran away.

Sam looked calmly around. No one said anything or made a move toward him He holstered his weapon and walked to the other side of his horse. He slung his leg over the bare back of the animal and rode slowly down the street. He felt many eyes following his progress and penetrating his back.

It took him fifteen minutes to get to the north edge of the town. People were looking and pointing at him all the way.

Sam kicked up his mount as he left the outskirts of El Paso. The mountains to his left loomed even larger.

Ten minutes out of town he heard horses riding hard behind him. He turned and saw five men on his trail. One of them was the eye bulging man who had swallowed his tobacco. He spurred the horse across the river and headed for the foothills. The five riders followed in hot pursuit.

He made it to the tall rocks and began weaving in and around them. When he got to an opening, he looked back at his pursuers. He saw only three of them following behind. Where were the other two?

Now he would have to be more aware. He was on their turf and it was not familiar to him. They didn't seem to be in much of a hurry to catch up with him.

It was the same way most of the day. They had tracked and followed him relentlessly. It was getting close to dusk with the sun going down over the distant mountain peaks. The oncoming darkness made it harder for him to maneuver.

Sam rounded a rock and turned to look back at his trackers. When he did a resounding thud to the side of his temple knocked him off his horse. He fell hard into a pile of rocks. A sharp pain went through his body as he hit the rocks on his left shoulder. The last thing he remembered was someone slapping the paint on his haunches and watching him run away. Then someone struck him again and he was unconscious.

Sometime later, he began to come around enough to feel his head throbbing. He could see the flicker of low flames and hear muffled voices and nervous laughter. He could not make out what they were saying. He tried to get to his feet and discovered his hands were tied behind his back. His head was aching and his vision was blurred. What were they going to do with him?

He passed out again from the pain in his head. He woke again sometime later and heard drunken laughter coming from near the fire. His chin dropped to his chest and he went out again.

When he woke again the fire was out. He could only see silhouettes of mounds around where the fire had been. One man sat facing him with a rifle across his lap. Sam could tell by the drooping of his head that he was also asleep. When Sam was fully alert, he found he was leaning with his back against two large boulders. He moved his hands and found them still tied behind him. He struggled to get freed but the harder he pulled, the tighter his bonds became. The circulation was being cut off and his hands were getting really numb. He twisted and turned in an effort to free himself. He would stop and rest his hands and sore shoulder until the pain subsided, then try again, to no avail.

It was on one of these periods of rest that he felt someone slide a hand between the two boulders. Whoever it was felt of his swollen hands and then withdrew. After another moment, the hand reached in again, this time it was wielding a knife. He felt his numb hands fall loosely to the ground as the thong was cut from them.

Sam sat motionless, not daring to move and be seen. He looked in the direction of his captors and none of had moved. They were unaware of his freedom.

He rolled to his right side and painfully, slowly staggered to his feet. His head throbbed again as he worked to control his balance. Out of the darkness he saw a hand extend and with a crooked finger beckoned him to follow. He looked back at his enemies, and, slowly took steps to follow his helper.

Sam continued to stagger along behind a shadow throughout the dark night. There was no bright moon to guide him and he could not get a good look at the person he was following. It seemed like he had walked through the foothills for hours.

His guide began to climb upward over rocks to a higher elevation. He did not know where he was being led, but he went along like a puppy with a new master. Up and up, they climbed for another hour. Suddenly, his host was gone and he could see the low flicker of a flame through an opening leading into to a huge cavern. It was hidden from view by an outcropping of rocks.

He climbed onto a ledge and cautiously entered into the cave. Who brought him here? How did they know he needed help?

Sam fell to his knees and thanked the Lord for sending an angel to him once again.

As dawn was breaking over El Paso, Sam watched five riders slowly make their way to the southeast and back toward the border town of El Paso. They were all slumped over in their saddles, probably suffering from throbbing heads much like Sam. While he watched he heard the nicker of a horse.

He stared into the depths of the cavern and saw a familiar paint pony step out of the dark shadows. His bag of booty was still hanging from its sides.

How? Who?

He found another fire prepared and ready to light. With his knife and flint, surprisingly the one who had tied his hands didn't take them. Sam made a fire for coffee.

He decided to rest for the day and sleep another night before moving on. His head was still hurting and so was the wound on his arm and his hands.

He didn't stray too far away from his hideaway. He did make short forays looking for signs of the guardian angel. He found none.

His head and shoulder had improved with a day of rest and a good night of sound sleep. After the Indian pony had reappeared, Sam had found his Sharps and his revolver, complete with gun belt and holster. They were leaning neatly against the inside wall of the cave, near the entrance.

Checking the eastern horizon toward the town of El Paso and seeing no one, he mounted up and slowly picked his way down the mountainside. He rode back toward the Rio Grande River.

When he looked back to the cave, he knew why the men had not tried to find him. There were numerous caverns on the eastern slope of the mountains. Some were natural caverns. Others were carved by a previous culture. He turned north at the river and rode out of Texas

SIX

The nursing child will play by the hole of the cobra, and the weaned child will put his hand on the viper's den.   Isaiah 8:11

The terrain in New Mexico territory did not change much. It was the same dry mesquite and cactus covered land he had just left in Texas.

Sam had mixed emotions about leaving the Lone Star State. It had been like the Promised Land to him. After four long years of turmoil and death, in a war that was called civil, Texas was a mild oasis.

He had been through trials and tribulations in the last year. First Sam had lost his friend Castile in the

Chisos Mountains. Then he had joined his friends in a battle with rustlers
 After that he was wounded and pursued by a hostile band of Apache.

Sam put his fingers to the medallion that had been given to him by the Apache war chief, Victorio. He nearly lost it along with his life when he was captured by outlaws from El Paso.

Someone or something had rescued him. Twice he had been brought to a cavern and taken care of by an unseen force. Only once had he gotten a glimpse of a beckoning finger. Whatever it was, Sam gave all the due to his Lord and Savior Jesus Christ. He said a silent prayer of thanksgiving.

The landscape began to change. There were arroyos and gullies on both sides of the river.

After Sam had followed the river for a couple of hours, he came upon a sign. Reaching down from his mount, he brushed away the sand straining to make it out. The words were written on a weathered and worn slab of timber that was attached to a fence post. Sam had to turn the pinto and ride back some distance to make out what it said. It read Las Cruces 20 miles.

It was the first sign of civilization Sam had seen since leaving El Paso. It did not make him particularly happy. All of his encounters with people lately, had left him disillusioned.

Sam rode on, traveling in and out of arroyos, trying to keep the river in sight.

About midday he stopped in one of the high walled gullies to rest and water the pinto. He found shade and sat for a while giving the horse a break.

He removed a can of peaches that had been salvaged by whoever had rounded up his pony. He slowly savored every bite from the large can draining every drop of the thick sweet juice. It was a treat he had last tasted in a farm house in Mississippi. He thought about the friends he had traveled with and wondered what they were doing.

When he stood up and prepared to mount his horse, the paint pony nickered and laid his ears back. He had heard something. Sam stopped and listened. He heard not a sound in the quiet desert air. He looked up and down the arroyo and saw nothing moving. Slowly he lifted the Sharps to a ready position and waited. Nothing happened.

Maybe the horse just thought he heard something. Sam knew better. Horses were very sensitive to sounds.

He mounted and rode warily on to the north. He wanted to get along to the snowcapped mountains. There were fewer people there and being alone meant true solitude.

After an hour his tension had relaxed and he was again concentrating on the river. He took his time. He was not going to be in a hurry to see people again. Up and down, in and out of several gullies he rode.

He only saw the Rio Grande when he was on high ground now. Sometimes the arroyos followed close to the river bank, other times they took him nearly out of sight of the water.

It was one of the times, when not in sight of the river, that the horse pulled up and once again laid back his ears. He snorted and had a wild frightened look in his eyes. He began to shake his head up and down and paw at the ground with his forefoot.

Sam suddenly saw and heard what the pony had detected. A sidewinder was coiled on a rock just about head high cooling in the shade under the overhang. Its tail was vibrating in the quiet desert calm, creating a loud clacking noise. Pulling hard on the reins, Sam tried to turn the paint out of harm's way.

It was too late. The short, fat reptilian monster had stopped shaking its tail and in a lightning fast move, lunged at Sam.

Sam swung the Sharps in an attempt to divert the reptile's strike. He caught it midway between the head and tail. The snake fell, but with its mouth wide open, it hit Sam in the calf of his left leg. The fangs drove deep into his flesh.

The Indian pony neighed loudly and reared on its hind legs. Sam went over backwards and fell hard on the bitten leg. He could feel the bone snap at the place where the sidewinder had injected venom into the leg. The Sharps left his hand and slid across the rocks out of his reach.

Through the pain Sam heard the sound of hooves galloping away. With a blurring vision, he watched the sidewinder slither away across the hot desert sand, leaving tracks. He thought the snake had the horns of Satan protruding above its eyes. It was only the scales that a sidewinder was equipped with to keep sand out of its eyes as it buried itself in the sand hiding from potential prey.

When his eyes opened again he wasn't sure where he was. It was very quiet and a soft breeze cooled his perspiring, feverish face. He saw and reached for his floppy hat to protect his head from the sun.

Where am I? What happened?

He felt the excruciating pain in his leg and remembered being bitten by a snake. He tried to move his leg to see how bad it was, but his leg wouldn't move. Must get to the river.

Sam proceeded to try to drag himself toward the Rio Grande. The pain in his leg made it hard for him to crawl along. He seemed to go only inches and pass out. Each time he woke he would manage to drag himself a few inches more.

Which way is the water? Sun… look for the sun… West… that's where the river is.

He rolled onto his back and with his knife cut the buckskin pants off at the knees. With the pain it was a slow process

Got to make a tourniquet.

He tied the pant leg just above his knee to try and stop the venom from getting to his heart.
When he cinched it tight, the pain from the broken leg bone put him out again.

The hot sun was still bearing down on him when he came to. He rolled to his belly and began to crawl again dragging the bad leg.

Keep moving… got to have water.

He was determined to get to the river, if only inches at a time.

Can't die …. Get to the mountain… Horse. Where is my horse?

Sam began to hallucinate, and he passed out again.

Peaches… need more peaches.

He crawled inch by inch in his delirium, in and out of consciousness

Awake again, he crawled more frantically now. He was beginning to go upward out of the arroyo.

Flat ground now… I can make it.

On his back again he woke staring at the red ball in the sky. He blinked in the brightness. Something was moving in the sunlight. He felt something on his face. Sam swatted at his face and passed out.

Still on his back, he opened his eyes. This time, the sun was subdued as it moved to the western horizon. He saw movement and felt something touching him. It was the paint pony. It was standing over him, dangling the reins down to touch his face.

Sam grabbed hold of the reins and tried to pull himself up, but he was too weak. His leg was swollen to twice its normal size. He did not dare loosen the tourniquet. He passed out from the pain once more, but held onto the reins as if his life depended on it.

It was dusk when Sam woke again. With both hands he pulled down on the reins. Gradually, he was able to get his right foot under him, being careful not to step down on his snake bitten broken leg. He pushed and pulled until he was standing on one foot. He leaned against the pony and rested for what seemed a long time. Sam needed to make it to the river. He needed water.

Where am I? Where is Elizabeth?

Elizabeth was the girl he was to marry back in Mississippi. She had been murdered by marauders, along with her parents.

Sam was getting more delirious. The pain in his leg was becoming unbearable. Without realizing what he was doing, he stepped down on his bad leg. A scream came up from his throat. Down he went again in an unconscious heap.

He was hallucinating again. The horse was dancing and laughing at him, pulling at him with the reins still clutched in his hand. Flames swirled around him and then suddenly he was under a waterfall. How peaceful. It must be heaven. Cool clear water rushed over his head and down his face. Men were running, cannons firing. Explosions. Bodies flying. Run for the trees. Can't run, leg hurts too bad. Water… Water…. Elizabeth…Cold cloth… Feels good….Knife… Leg… Pain… Sleep…. Fire-light.

Sam woke once more and did see firelight blinking somewhere nearby. It was dark and someone moved quietly around the flickering flames of a fire. He went to sleep again, waking several times during the night. Then the only light he saw was a sky abundantly clad with stars. The moon was only a slim sliver, making the milky-way, seem even brighter.

The pain in his leg had eased and his mind was beginning to clear. He still dreamed constantly of times gone by.

How long have I been here? How did I get here?

In the glow of the starlight, he could make out the reflection of a rippling stream of water.

Sam slept again until the sun was above the eastern horizon. He woke and smelled smoke from a fire. There was another odor he was not familiar with. He licked his parched lips, and for the first time since the encounter with the sidewinder, felt hunger.

Raising himself up on one elbow he saw his still swollen left leg. It had gone down dramatically since he last remembered seeing it. There were four mesquite limbs spaced equally around his leg from his knee to his ankle. On the side of his calf where the pit viper had struck were two cross marks made with a sharp blade. Someone had removed the venom and saved his life.

He tried to get to his feet, but became light headed and fell back to a prone position. He lay very still with his eyes closed, waiting for the world to stop spinning. He dozed again. Between the snake bite, the broken leg and no food he had become very weak.

He was dreaming again that he was in a Mississippi swamp hiding from the war. Like now, he had been days without food... Elizabeth... her young beautiful face kept coming back to him, but this time her vision kept being replaced with that of a dark skinned young woman, confusing him, interrupting his dream. Elizabeth's blond flowing hair was replaced with black braids

A hand on his shoulder began gently shaking him. He opened his eyes and saw a blurred outline. It was the dark skin beauty from his dream. Moving his head from side to side, he opened and closed his eyes, trying to clear his vision by blinking.

The young Indian woman was holding onto a short handled gourd that had been made into a bowl. It contained a steaming odorous liquid. The odor he had detected earlier in one of his moments of being awake.

"You eat!" The vision spoke to him.

Sam slowly raised himself onto one elbow. The woman held the cup to his lips and he took a small taste of the broth, not recognizing the taste. It was hot, but felt good going down his throat. After several small gulps, he laid back and closed his eyes again. This time his dream had only the face of an Indian maiden. He slept more peaceful. The nightmares were going away.

When his eyes opened again the maiden was kneeling at his side. She had both hands cupped around the hot steaming broth. Holding the bowl to his lips, she again fed him the healing concoction.

"Who are you? Where did you come from?" Sam spoke in a hoarse, raspy voice. He was very weak.

"You eat," was her only reply. This time Sam consumed all of the liquid before falling back in to a restful sleep.

It was dusk the next time he woke up. He could make out two shadows near the fire. They both sat with legs crossed and talked softly across the low flame. One of them was the young maiden. It was hard for Sam to make out the other form. It appeared much taller than she and sat with arms folded across his chest.

He must be a proud man.

Sam moved slightly and the action alerted the two fireside figures. The maiden got to her feet and walked quickly to his side. She brought the bowl with her once again.

He held his hand up palm toward her in a motion to stop her.

"Who are you?"

The girl stopped short, a puzzled look on her face.

"You eat now."

"No ... Who are you?" Sam was adamant.

"I am Spotted Fawn, I am Tonkawa."

"Who is he?" Sam looked in the direction of the fire.

"That is Walks Like a Coyote. He is my grandfather. He is father of Castile. Castile my uncle. Walking Dog is my Father. Walking Dog brother of Castile. Both go to be with Wolf in the sky. Happy hunting ground.

"Why are you here? How did you find me?" Sam asked still confused.

"Castile send word to Walks Like a Coyote, 'Take care of my friend.' Grandfather is old...I help." She was stern in her reply and the expression on her face. "Find you in cave. We hide from Apache, come when they not around."

"You're the one! You have been helping me." He looked at her in amazement.

She rose quickly and went to join Walks Like a Coyote. They continued their quiet conversation.

Sam went back to sleep. His last thoughts as he closed his eyes were about his true friend Castile.

After several days of broth, Spotted Fawn began to feed Sam small game roasted over the hot coals. He never questioned what it was. His body was craving food. The snake venom was gone from his body and his strength was returning day by day.

He asked the maiden how long it had been since they found him. Her only reply was.

"Many moons." She spoke only when he asked a question. She was shy and quiet.

Walks Like a Coyote was even quieter. He spoke only to Spotted Fawn and then only when spoken to. It was difficult for Sam to determine how old the man was. He appeared to show signs of age and frailty, even though his hair was jet black. Sam could see that it was difficult for him to walk very far. Yet he had traveled far on foot looking after his son's friend.

...

Sam's leg had begun to heal. He could stand and hop around on his good one. As he began to slowly move around the camp, he found the Sharps rifle he had lost.

Hobbled near the river bank was the paint pony who had tried to save him. He eyed Sam curiously when he approached.

Sam persistently tried every day to mount the horse. After a week, he managed to put enough weight on his splinted leg to throw his right one over. He sat proudly on the pinto's back, looking down at the two Tonkawa who watched curiously.

The Tonkawa were a nation who traveled only on foot or by canoe. They did not understand this fascination for a four legged animal to ride.

Sam was now ready to resume his journey up the Rio Grande. He mounted and rode out in the direction of Las Cruces, stopping to see if his new companions were following. He once again thanked the Lord for sending someone to help him along the way.

Spotted Fawn and Walks Like a Coyote walked alongside him. Since he now knew who they were there was no need to follow and watch from a distance.

SEVEN

> The steps of a man are established by the Lord, And He delights in his way. When he falls, he will not be hurled headlong. Because the Lord is the one who holds his hand. I have been young and now I am old, Yet I have not seen the righteous forsaken Or his descendants begging bread.
> Psalms 37:23-25

Spotted Fawn had been in the New Mexico Territory one other time. When she was very young the Tonkawa had made a journey to this strange land. She vaguely remembered some of the landscape around her. It was not unlike Texas.

Walks Like a Coyote remembered it too. It had been a time of escape for his tribe. The Apache had driven them out of their homeland in south Texas when he was much younger. It was only for a short time but it weighed heavily on his memory.

The people the Tonkawa knew only as the white ones had continually multiplied and spread westward across the vast lands of Texas. Many of the renegade Apache had been killed or scattered by them, freeing the land for the Tonkawa's return. They came home to their own land and many of them became scouts for the army. Some of them scouted for Union troops and others for the Confederacy. When the war had ended the Tonkawa gladly helped the Texas Rangers drive out more of the Apache.

Walks Like a Coyote and Spotted Fawn were in and out of the trail that Sam traveled along the river. Sometimes they were with him and other times they simply disappeared into the caliche countryside. Sometimes one of them would reappear with a rabbit or some other kind of small game. Sometimes Walks Like a Coyote would have a dead sidewinder thrown over one of his shoulders. Sam knew he would have meat of some kind to hang on a fire spit in the evening.

It was a time of familiarity for the three of them. They were beginning to get used to each other being around the fire and sharing food and time together. Walks Like a Coyote still did not speak the white man's language. He did give Sam an occasional answer through his granddaughter. Sam never pushed him, but allowed him time to sit quietly and gaze into the starry sky. It was as though he were looking for something in the heavens.

Spotted Fawn was also a quiet one. Like her grandfather she spent a lot of time in thought. She had learned to speak quite good white man's tongue from her uncle and Tonkawa chieftain Castile.

At night, when the fire had burned down to a warm ash, the two with red skin would disappear into the night while Sam lay on his saddle next to the fireside. He always awoke to see Spotted Fawn rekindling the fire. On a few occasion Walks Like a Coyote came into camp with eggs in both hands. Some were small quail eggs and some from the nest of a prairie chicken. It did not matter to Sam. He enjoyed them all. His traveling companions did not drink the hot black elixir of the white man. Spotted Fawn had learned how to make the foul tasting liquid for Sam in the mornings but turned her nose up at the smell. He would sip the coffee slowly and lick his lips in pleasure just to taunt her. Spotted Fawn could only shake her head in disgust. Walks Like a Coyote would show no emotion.

The white man who wanted to be alone in the mountains was finding himself becoming fond of the beautiful young red woman. When the two of them were alone, he felt a closeness that he had not experienced in a long while. When she departed from him he longed to see her. The last time he felt this way about a woman was with a beautiful young blond girl called Elizabeth. That seemed so long ago in a faraway land.

Sam found himself watching as the buckskin clad maiden dipped a blue porcelain coffee pot into the

Rio Grande River. She did it just to please him. She knew he watched and it pleased her.

---...---

They had traversed the New Mexico part of the Rio Grande for two weeks. Sam knew he should be in a hurry to get to the Colorado Territory, but he was enjoying this time of calm with Spotted Fawn and Walks Like a Coyote.

Sam had been through so much pain and turmoil in the recent weeks and his body had suffered much from arrows, a snake bite, and a broken leg. He convinced himself he needed this time to mend.

He opened his eyes one morning to see Spotted Fawn adding mesquite limbs to a smoldering fire. He smiled at her back and turned to look for the man who had brought him eggs for two weeks. There was no one there.

Sam yawned and stretched slowly before rising to his feet. There was still some pain in his leg that had been broken and snake bit. He walked tenderly and with a slight limp toward the fire. The coffee pot was just beginning to gurgle so he would have to wait. He smiled at Spotted Fawn and turned to look to the rocks around them. The Indian maiden saw the concern in Sam's eyes and followed his gaze to the rocks for Walks Like a Coyote. There still was no sign of her grandfather.

Sam gathered his Sharps from near his bedroll and cautiously stepped toward the opening where he expected to see the old man. Walks Like a Coyote stepped out and grunted impatiently at the white man. In his hands were six prairie chickens eggs. He turned to his granddaughter and mumbled something in his native tongue.

She spoke to him softly and turned to the fire. The black brew was done and she poured a cup for Sam. He could see she was trying to hide her concern for the old one, but she did not speak of it.

As they left the camp, Spotted Fawn walked closely with her grandfather. She spoke to him quietly but he ignored her concern for him. He crossed his arms across his chest and walked proudly along.

Sam kept turning to watch the old man as he strode proudly along the banks of the Rio Grande. Spotted Fawn walked behind and close to Walks Like a Coyote. He stumbled at times but regained his balance and stomped along. He wanted no help, especially from a young woman.

---·· ·---

When the sky was turning to gray and the sun was hovering over the western horizon Sam pulled rein in a clump of mesquite shrouded by boulders.

They had bypassed Los Cruces and had come to a place where the river widened. It was near to being a lake.

The mesquites were turning from trees to a smaller bush as they ventured into a desert terrain. There was more Yucca and cactus.

Sam gathered mesquite sticks and started a small fire. Spotted Fawn walked slowly into the flickering fire light and dropped a small animal carcass onto the ground

"I am concerned for Walks Like a Coyote. He is old and it is near his time to go to the lair of the wolf." She looked at Sam with a hollow fear in her eyes.

Sam knew that this young woman loved her grandfather dearly. He also knew it was not the Tonkawa way to show emotion. She turned and began to prepare the meat for the fire. Sam took the coffeepot to the river for water. This would be his last pot until he could make it back into the world of the white man.

Walks Like a Coyote, was sitting cross- legged on the opposite side of the river. As Sam dipped the pot he saw the old one seated in front of a small flickering fire. His arms were raised and he made a low soft chanting sound to the starlit sky.

Sam filled the pot and walked quietly back to the fire where Spotted Fawn waited. That night she slept opposite him across the dying embers.

Sam understood the ways of the red man from his time with Castile. He knew that all he could do was to be there for Spotted Fawn when the time came.

He reached for his Bible and clutching it to his breast prayed for Spotted Fawn and the old brave Walks Like a Coyote. He asked God to forgive them their beliefs and accept the old one to his bosom.

He slept peacefully knowing that God was with him and would guide him along the way.

There was no coffee pot on the fire when Sam woke. Spotted Fawn was standing away from the fire gazing toward the river. She was feeling something new to her. At least it was new and different from her teaching. Red women were taught to never show their emotions. How could she explain, the tear running down her cheek.

She felt Sam's movement behind her and quickly wiped her cheek. She did not want him to see weakness in her. Looking down she quickly skirted around Sam and went to the fire.

Walks Like a Coyote did not come to the fire that day.

Sam and Spotted Fawn continued on the way to Colorado Territory. She was alone now with no one to share her language and beliefs. She would continue as her Uncle Castile had instructed her grandfather from the other side. Take care of the white man who had been his friend. Now she must commit her life to watching after Sam Raines. It was the way of the Tonkawa.

"I go with you now." She spoke quietly to Sam, "I watch out for you now."

Sam's first impulse was to say he didn't need anybody to take care of him. He silently considered the last three months.

"I will take you along till we find some of your people." He wasn't sure if the Tonkawa had left some of their people in the New Mexico territory. There were other friendly tribes. Surely one of them would take her in.

"We go to Colorado." Without thinking Sam invited her along on his trek up the Rio Grande River.

"You ride horse with me Spotted Fawn," He told her as they were breaking camp.

"I walk," she explained.

"You ride, walk too slow. We must get to mountain. Snow... White powder cover mountains.

"I walk! Not like horse." For the first time fear was in her eyes. "You ride horse. I walk. It is way of Tonkawa."

Sam mounted the horse and rode out along the river bank. Spotted Fawn followed along behind. He spurred the horse to a fast walk. She quickened her pace to keep up.

When she thought Sam was not looking she stopped and scanned the trail behind them; then ran to catch up. There was no sign of Walks Like a Coyote. She lowered her head and followed in the tracks of Sam's horse. She wiped her cheek on the back of her hand.

The Rio Grande widened again into a small lake. Sam pulled rein and once more dismounted on the bank of the river. He did not remove the saddle from his horse.

When Spotted Fawn walked into the cluster of mesquite Sam pointed to the animal. "You take horse to water."

She stopped suddenly and looked at Sam in amazement. She looked at the horse. "You horse... You take horse."

"You brave woman... You watch for me. Castile say you watch for me. You take horse. You ride horse"

Spotted Fawn stepped cautiously to the side of the horse. She walked around and looked quizzically at the four legged monster.

"How take horse to water?"

"Grab him by the reins" he pointed, "Reins... Hold reins, throw leg over." He pointed upward. "Throw over" Sam put her hand onto the reins.

"You can do it." He pointed to the mane on the horse's neck.

As Spotted Fawn touched the mane, the horse turned to look curiously at her. She stepped away.

"He won't hurt you. Rub his neck." Sam was enjoying her predicament.

Spotted Fawn cautiously rubbed along the horse's neck causing a quiver in his withers. She jumped back frightened by the reflex.

"He likes you." Sam laughed.

After twenty minutes she was becoming less frightened and Spotted Fawn placed her hands as she had seen Sam do many times. She pulled hard on the mane, stumbled, and toppled over backwards.

Sam rushed quickly to her side and lifted her off the ground. "You try again."

Fawn looked at him, rubbing her backside

"Try again!" You can do it."

Fawn walked slowly back to the pinto. "You help. Horse to big."

Sam cupped his hands together. "Step in my hands."

Fawn put her left foot into Sam's hands watching him closely.

He lifted her up and slid her onto the back of the horse.

"Tomorrow you ride."

"I ride!" Spotted Fawn beamed at Sam, proud of her accomplishment.

EIGHT

Even though I walk through the valley of the shadow of death. I
fear no evil; for Thou art with me;
Thy rod and Thy staff, they comfort me. Thou dost prepare a
table in the presence of my enemies; Thou hast anointed my
head with oil; My cup overflows. Psalm 23:4-5

The two of them rode north the following morning. Spotted Fawn was not as ready to mount the four legged creature as she thought she was the day before. Sam moved his foot forward and reached out to take her hand. Cautiously she raised her right leg and waited for Sam to lift her.. Sam pulled her up and swung her small light body onto the horse behind him. Spotted Fawn wrapped both arms around his middle and clasping her hands together hung on for dear life.

Sam smiled to himself at her discomfort. Her moccasin clad feet dug deep into the animal's haunches causing him to jump forward and gallop off along the river bank. Sam laughed and pulled back on the reins slowing the horse to a walk.

They were about two miles south of the settlement at San Antonio by mid-afternoon. Sam knew that Spotted Fawn was ready for a rest even though she said nothing. He pulled rein alongside the bank of the Rio Grande and reached his arm around behind her back. She held his arm and slid slowly to the ground. Spotted Fawn crept to the river with stooped shoulders and waded into the clear cold water.

Sam had stopped earlier than he normally would to give the young maiden a rest from the rough bouncing ride. That and he wanted to wander into the settlement and try to find coffee. He hated to leave the girl alone, but knew she was capable of taking care of herself. She had been on her own for a long time while watching out for him. Her grandfather Walks Like a Coyote had been with her along the way but he had been ailing and needed much help.

He dismounted and allowed the horse to take a long cool drink. The water seemed to be running faster and colder at this spot. Sam filled his canteen and spoke to Spotted Fawn.

"I am going into San Antonio to find coffee and maybe some flour and bacon." Sam motioned in the direction of the town. San Antonio, New Mexico Territory was a much smaller version of its sister city San Antonio, Texas

"I stay." Spotted Fawn answered as he had expected.

He rode out and stopped upstream to look over his shoulder. Spotted Fawn was still waist deep in the flowing waters of the Rio Grande. Sam continued on his way and came to the edge of a small village late in the afternoon. There was a small trading post on the river bank. The only activity he saw was a couple of Indians seated on grain bags on the front porch of an old adobe structure.

As Sam approached a man stepped out the front door and lit four lanterns hanging under a worn and dilapidated extension. The man only glanced at Sam then turned and walked back inside.

Sam stepped down and tied the horse to a corner post of the old porch. He walked one step up and entered where the lantern lighter had gone. When he was inside he saw two other men seated at a table against a back wall. They two of them looked up, tipped their head, and went back to their conversation.

The man who had lit the lanterns spoke to Sam.

'Help you mister?"

"Got any coffee? Could use some flour and bacon too," Sam answered the man while watching the two seated at the table.

"Stranger in these parts, ain't you?" the proprietor asked.

"Yep," Sam replied.

"Don't get too many strangers around here. Where you headed?"

"Colorado territory." Sam was terse in his response.

"Got some coffee. Little chunk of bacon? Got no flour though." The man sensed Sam didn't want to talk and went back to tending to his business.

The two seated men got to their feet and walked across the room. "How much for the steaks George?" One asked.

"Two bits apiece Mr. Maxwell." He held out his hand and the man gave him a dollar.

"Going to Colorado territory are you?" The man paying asked.

"Yessir, that's my plan." Sam answered.

"I'm Lucien Maxwell. My friend here is Kit Carson. I didn't get your name."

"I'm Sam Raines, Mr. Maxwell. How do you do Mr. Carson." He put out his hand and both shook his hand vigorously.

"Comancheros, around these parts. Better be careful." It was Kit Carson who warned him.

"Comancheros? They Indians?" Sam queried the two. He had never heard that name.

"Some. A few are renegade Apache and Comanche. Most are white outlaws from the war. Some are Mexicans. All are thieving murdering pole cats. Watch yourself through here."

"Thank you Mister Carson…Mister Maxwell." Sam took a bag from George the proprietor and walked quietly out into the dark night air.

———— ….. ————

A chill moved up Sam's spine as he turned his horse to ride back along the river. He had seen no one nor signs of anyone in days.

It was dark with only a half moon to guide him as he approached the spot where he thought he had left Spotted Fawn. There was no fire to guide him but he was sure of the place. It did not bother him because she was not about. She was with him for months without him knowing she was there. He built a small fire and made a pot of coffee. She would see the flames and come to the camp.

Sam finished off the last cup and staked his horse, gazing toward the river as he did so. He laid his head back on the ground and drifted off to sleep.

He expected to see Spotted Fawn puttering around the fire when he woke. She was not there. Sam looked around curiously, then shrugged his shoulder and went to the river to retrieve coffee water. As he approached the river bank he saw something he had not seen in the dark of night. There were hoof prints all over the bank. Many horses had been there. Where is Spotted Fawn?

He pulled his side gun and began backing away from the river. His senses had come to full alert. He looked up and down the river and across to the other side. There were tracks on the other bank too. Backing into the mesquite he realized, he had a tight grip with both his hands, one on a six gun, the other one on the coffee pot.

He made it to his horse, dropping the pot and picking up his Sharps. Holstering the six gun Sam moved cautiously back toward the river. He stopped and knelt while still in the brush. His eyes went to the other side of the river scanning in all directions. Twenty yards up the river he saw something out of place. He crawled slowly along the river's edge keeping the mesquite between him and the water. When he had crept twenty yards he stopped and stared across the river. There were two sets of hoofs with two distinctive tracks between them. Someone had been dragged from the water and a long distance across the desert sands. The tracks were followed by as many as twenty horses.

"Please God… Keep her safe."
 Sam spoke the prayer out loud as he began to back track to where he left his horse. He mounted his animal with shaky hands, and then quickly rode full tilt across the Rio Grande.

Sam's mind went back to the conversation he had with Lucien Maxwell and Kit Carson. Comanchero! They had a full night head start on him. What would he do when he caught up with them? He was one man. They were at least twenty.

He rode west into the hot desert sun. After an hour of hard riding Sam realized he could not keep up this pace for long. He was going deep into the great Chihuahua Desert. He had been in the desert since leaving Texas but always along the banks of the Rio Grande River.

Now as he moved westward away from that body of water it was becoming a different land. The mesquite that grew along the river bank had given way to a land dotted with cactus and other plants he did not recognize. There was no shade from the searing sun. There were Gila's and Sidewinders everywhere.

It was not hard to track the men who had taken Spotted Fawn from him. They were not trying to hide their trail. They were many and were a hard callous bunch of outlaws who feared no one. They had the run of this country and did whatever pleased them. They robbed, killed, ran rampant over small settlements and stole their women at will. The captive women were passed around amongst them until they were no longer wanted, then left to die or be killed. By this time death was an escape from the horror at the hands of the Comanchero.

By the day's end the terrain was beginning to increase in elevation. Sam was moving into the foothills of a mountain range. Unlike the Chisos Mountains of the Big Bend, this range remained dry and arid. There was only an occasional Pinion tree. The only other shade to be found was under huge hot boulders.

Sam stopped and dismounted under an outcropping of jagged rock with one tree that looked as if it had been struck by lightning. He watered his horse and himself sparingly. He had not seen water since leaving the river.

His friend Castile had taught him well. He knew where to find water or survive without it. This was going to be one of those times. He stumbled into the foothills pulling his horse along behind him.

It was getting on to near dusk and the sun was slipping down behind the western mountain peaks. Sam noticed that the many tracks he followed were becoming fresher. He thought they had traveled throughout the night, but it seemed they had stopped and slept. What about Spotted Fawn? Had they harmed her?

Sam felt a rapid increase in his heart beat. He must save this redskin maiden. He must save this beautiful Spotted Fawn. He must free her from the pagan beliefs of her people and introduce her to his God. Sam knew now that he would wed Spotted Fawn. He was in love with her and wanted to spend the rest of his life with her by his side.

As he threaded his way through the rocks Sam detected the slightest smell of smoke.
He guardedly worked his way further along until he began to hear voices. They were loud boisterous sounds. Some were English, some Spanish, and some a mixture of both languages.

He left his horse under the edge of an overhanging rock and crept to where the voices were coming from. There was no need to be quiet. The men he pursued could not have cared less. Sam got within sight of a fire and sat trying to determine where all his enemies were situated. There were three fires going in a large circle, surrounded completely by boulders. There were four lean-to structures built against the rock walls on the outer perimeter. Nearly all the men he saw wore sombreros and they all had bandoleers crisscrossed over their chest. They were laughing and passing jugs around from one to the other.

Across the way Sam spotted a man seated high up on a boulder with his back to the encampment. He had a rifle lying across his lap. Horses! He must be watching horses.

In the flickering of the firelight Sam picked out several women laughing together with the outlaws and passing whiskey jugs and food around to them. It was hard to tell if the women were captives or camp followers who cooked and cared for this cruel bunch. He watched and searched the camp for an hour trying to locate Spotted Fawn. Where do they have her? Suddenly across one of the fires, seated back between two of the boulders he made out the faint outline of what appeared to be a woman clad in buckskins. He could not make out her facial features, but it looked as if her hands were tied behind her back.

From where Sam watched the figure it was a hundred feet to where she sat. He would have to circle around the camp and try to locate her position. Then he could free her hands as she had once freed his.

He began inching his way, struggling over and around boulders. Sometimes he was in sight of the camp and sometimes twenty yards away behind boulders. It was taking a long time to make his way around the encampment. Some of the outlaws had fallen asleep around the fires. Others had moved away into the lean-tos with their women. Sam finally found a crevice half way round the circle and looked in the direction of the one place he thought was where he had seen Spotted Fawn. She was gone!

At that instant he saw movement across the circle and above him.

There was a blood curdling scream and the outlaw, who had been watching the horses, toppled from his perch into one of the fires. At the same moment three very large gray wolves entered the camp from three different locations. They began to attack the outlaws, mauling and tearing at their throats. A lone figure appeared above Sam where the lookout had been. He wore a wolf skin over his shoulders and head and war paint covered his face and body.

Out of the corner of his eye Sam saw a fleeting image dart away from the camp in the direction of his horse.

He looked back to the encampment in time to see several of the outlaws firing rapidly, cutting down the three wolves. The painted warrior raised his hands to the sky and let out one last chilling war whoop. The Comancheros all turned and fired a volley of bullets into the brave's chest. He too toppled into the camp, but in a circle created by the three dying wolves. The warrior was Walks Like a Coyote.

Sam stood, stunned for a moment, then turned and ran into the dark night to find his horse and Spotted Fawn.

NINE

render decisions for many people; And they will hammer their
swords into plow shares and their spears into pruning hooks.
Nations will not lift up And He will judge between the nations,
and will sword against nation. And never again will they learn
war. Isaiah 2:4

Sam made his way swiftly to where he had left the horse. When he reached for the reins, Spotted Fawn stepped out of the shadows and wrapped both arms around his neck. She clung to him until he softly removed her embrace. He motioned that they must be on their way. He did not know if spotted Fawn knew who had freed her. He only knew that he would never speak of what he had seen.

The hour was approaching midnight as they mounted and rode silently back through the rocks to the east. Sam spurred the horse to a trot as they cleared the foothills. It was best to make time in the cool desert night air. He expected that the Comancheros would come thundering behind them at any time.

The mountain man kept checking over his shoulder and listening for the sounds of hoof beats. When the sun crept up into the eastern horizon, Sam saw in the distance a faint cloud of dust coming toward them. There were riders between them and the Rio Grande. It would not be the outlaw band. They would come from behind them. Spotted Fawn touched his arm and pointed to the dust cloud. Sam shook his head for yes, and then pulled the horse's head in their direction.

As the riders drew close, Sam saw they were union Calvary troops riding in a typical, straight line, military formation. At the head of the column was a man Sam had seen before. He had met him in a trading post at the San Antonio settlement. This time he was wearing a blue uniform with captain's bars on his shoulders.

The officer raised his right hand and the sergeant behind him yelled.

"Troop Ho…"

Sam had recognized Kit Carson as the commander of a sixty man troop of soldiers.

"Mornin Mister Raines." The captain addressed Sam. "Out for a morning ride?"

"You could say that… Spotted Fawn had a run in with some of your Comancheros."

Spotted Fawn turned away from the soldiers and buried her face in Sam's back.

"We heard they were close by. We're going to see if we can find them" Kit Carson spoke to Sam.

"Don't seem to be hiding from anybody. I don't think they'll be hard to find." Sam replied.

"Can you show us where they were, last you saw them?" The captain asked.

Sam felt the pull of Spotted Fawn. She did not want to go back to where her captives were holed up.

"You get somebody to take her to a safe place... I show you."

"Sergeant! Get two good men to take this lady to the fort and remember... She is a lady!" The captain gave instructions to his men.

Spotted Fawn did not want Sam to leave her, she held onto him tightly. He gently unclasped her hands.

"I'll be back." He looked deeply into her dark brown eyes.

Spotted Fawn saw the look of love in Sam's eyes. She shook her head up and down and went to where the two soldiers waited.

"Private Sims... You ride double with McDonald... Let the lady have your mount." The sergeant turned away from the two troopers and rode to come along side Captain Carson.

Sam watched as Spotted Fawn climbed aboard the army mount then turned and followed the sergeant.

Sam rode alongside Kit Carson at the front of the column. Like before, the desert sun blazed across a deep blue sky. It was hard for Sam to keep his eyes open through the glare. He had not slept or eaten for two days and his body was telling him it was time to stop. He closed his eyes and allowed the steady roll of the horse rock him to sleep. The rest of the troop rode in silence as they crossed the scorching Chihuahua desert.

The clacking sound of horse's hooves on rock brought Sam abruptly out of a deep sleep. He impulsively reached for his sidearm. Realizing where he was he wiped the sleep and sweat from his eyes. The sergeant passed him an open canteen.

The water was not cold but it satisfied the dryness in his throat.

It was late in the day and the sun was hovering over the mountain tops. Sam was beginning to feel a familiarity with the landscape. He saw the opening in the rocks where he had watched the Comancheros the day before. It seemed as if it had been a week.

Captain Carson, with hand signals, dispersed his men in a large arcing circle. They encompassed the entire camp site.

Again with hand signals the troop moved forward. They slowly moved in on the Comanchero encampment. There were no Comancheros. Except for fire rings and lean-tos there was no sign anyone had been there. Walks Like a Coyote, the three wolf carcasses and all the dead outlaws were gone.

It appeared to be the site of an ancient civilization. Had he brought them to the wrong place? Sam was sure he was in the right spot. He walked to where he had left his horse. It was the place he and Spotted Fawn had left from the night before.

"It's not the first time Sam." Kit Carson said. "Every time we think we have them…, they disappear. Sergeant set up camp and feed the men. We'll bed down here."

Sam found a spot in one of the lean-tos. He was too tired to eat and fell quickly to sleep. As he drifted off, his thoughts were of Spotted Fawn. In one of his dreams he saw Walks Like a Coyote along with three giant gray wolves rising into the arms of God. In another Spotted Fawn beckoned to him from a rising Rio Grande River.

Over a cup of coffee with Captain Carson the next morning, the conversation was about the Comancheros. The army troop was going to continue its pursuit of the outlaws. Sam was free to return to the river. The army fed him and provided him slivers of beef jerky for his trip to the fort. He wasted no time in mounting up and riding out of that place for the second time in two days.

Sam promised himself that Spotted Fawn would not leave his side again. By days end he would be with her once more. He rode into a huge orange ball and felt the searing heat reflecting off the desert floor. Sam loosed the reins and gave the horse his head. Both of them had rested and been watered and fed. It was going to be a slow arduous journey back across the hot sand.

Gila's scurried from rock to rock, stopping just long enough to stare at the passing pair of man and horse. Sidewinders slithering across the sand would stop and coil into a defensive posture at the sound of hoofs clicking on small pebbles. An occasional jack rabbit would freeze in position until the danger had passed. Sam would raise his canteen and salute the inhabitants of the dry arid Chihuahua Desert, then take a cool drink to sooth his parched tongue. He always provided a cupped hand full of water for the faithful animal that carried him back toward the Rio Grande.

---------- ..... ----------

Fort Craig was located on the west side of the river on a high sandy bank. On the east bank and three miles south of the fort was a small settlement called San Marcial.

The original outpost on this section of the Rio Grande was Fort Conrad. It was built eight miles upriver in eighteen fifty one. Unfortunately, it was inadvertently built on private land. Not only that, it was built adjacent to a mosquito infested river marsh. Many of the soldiers had contracted malaria. Fort Conrad was short lived.

In eighteen fifty four, Fort Craig was established thirty five miles south of Socorro. The fort was constructed with high thick foundations and high walls. There were twenty two rocks and adobe buildings within the walls encircling a large parade ground.

At the onset of the civil war an earthen dam was built around the fort and fortified with cannons.

When the confederate forces came up the

Rio Grande, they decided not to attack the fort. They met the union forces at Val Verde River Valley north of the fort and sent then into retreat. Continuing on to Albuquerque
And Santa Fe. The southerners captured both cities, before facing defeat at a place called Glorieta Pass.

The confederate army having lost its entire supply train, fled to the west and through the mountains, leaving weapons and supplies abandoned along the way, they made it back to Texas in splinter groups.

Fort Craig went back to the boredom of infrequent skirmishes with Indians and occasional attempts at destroying bands of outlaws like the Comancheros.

---------- ..... ----------

The cold water of the Rio Grande was beginning to rise when Captain Carson and his troop left Fort Craig in pursuit of the outlaw band. There was no concern for the fort. It had been built high above the river. There had been a long cold winter in the territory of Colorado and the snow melt coming down was overflowing the banks of the Rio Grande River. Sam could see the high walls of Fort Craig rising above the horizon. It was as if it were floating on a sea of clouds. When Sam had broken his leg and been bit by a venomous snake, he had seen visions like this. That was caused by delirium. The scene before him now was like a mirage riding on desert heat waves.

Drawing closer Sam could make out the wall of water rushing down the river and spreading over the east bank. There appeared to be a rush of activity outside the walls of the fort. No one paid much attention to him as he came close to the large double gate. The guards were directing civilians into the fort. Most of them were soaking wet as if they had swum the river.

"Halt Mister." One of the armed soldiers addressed him. "You from San Marcial?"

"San what?" Sam had never heard of that place.

"San Marcial… That little town down the river. It's flooded. Buildings wiped out. Some drowned. Injuns are bringing people cross the river in canoes. Colonel Danby's letting them stay in the fort."

Injuns! That word make Sam's mind begin to race. Spotted Fawn! He pulled his horse around and started for the open gate.

"Hey mister… Where you think you goin?" the guard yelled after him.

"To see the Colonel." Sam looked over his shoulder. "About an Injun!" He rode into the fort and across the parade ground. He saw an armed soldier standing at attention next to a heavy door. He pulled back on the reins.

"Where can I find Colonel Danby?" He asked the private.

"Over there sir!" the guard pointed across the parade ground to a smaller building. "This here is the guard house!"

Sam turned to look to where the man was pointing. He did not see the building. What he saw was a beautiful young Indian maiden running toward him. What he saw was Spotted Fawn. He dismounted his horse and ran to meet her.

TEN

In the beginning was the Word, and the Word was with God, and the Word was God. John 1;1

The moccasin and buckskin clad young woman jumped into the arms of the giant of a mountain man. With both arms around his neck and legs wrapped partially about his waist she laid her head upon his chest and held on tight.
Sam was not used to showing affection toward another, especially in the middle of a parade ground with others watching. Spotted Fawn had never expressed love for any other human, not even Walks Like a Coyote.

When Sam had pulled her arms loose and lowered her to the ground, both of them looked down at their feet in embarrassment.

Sam spoke first. "You okay?"

Spotted Fawn shook her head up and down, not looking into Sam's face.

"I guess we better find you a horse to ride." Sam spoke as they walked together toward the Fort Commanders office.

"Colonel Canby in his office?" He asked one of the two soldiers standing at attention on each side of the door.

"Sir Yes Sir!" Both guards answered in unison. Sam opened the heavy pine door and entered an outer room occupied by a small wooden desk with a large man in blue seated behind it.

"Who are you?" The man asked as Sam strode across to the desk

"Samson Raines, I need to talk to Colonel Canby, Captain Carson sent me."

The big sergeant recognized the name of Kit Carson "Yes sir, I'll tell the Colonel you're here."

Sam followed the man to the Colonels office and walked in behind him.

The sergeant started to speak and Sam interrupted. "Sam Raines, Colonel. Kit Carson asked me to report to you. He's gone after them Comancheros. Sam looked around and realized Spotted Fawn had not followed him into the building, "Said he would be back in two or three weeks."

Colonel Canby stood and spoke for the first time.
"Mister Raines, I'm Colonel Canby. Thanks for your report. Who are you?"
"I'm a man trying to get to the Colorado Territory. Them Comancheros took Spotted Fawn and I went after em, got her back. Captain Carson wanted me to show him where they were camped. They weren't there by the time we got back. Kit is goin to try to find em." Sam took a deep breath. "Don't normally talk this much."
"I see. I have met Spotted Fawn. Can't say I blame you for getting her back. You are welcome to stay as long as you want Mister Raines, may be a little crowded. San Marcial flooded out down river. Sergeant! Find quarters for Mister Raines and his … uh, lady." The Colonel shouted to the big man in blue.
"Yes, sir Colonel!"
"Uh… Colonel… Spotted Fawn is not my lady. She's my…Well we intend to get married" Sam stumbled over his words.
"I could use a horse… If you have one to spare." Sam quickly changed the subject.

"Sergeant ! Get Mister Raines a horse too!" He yelled again.
Sam turned and walked to the office door. He stopped and looked back at the Colonel with a quizzical expression as if to say something, but changed his mind. The Colonel was already seated looking at a paper in his hand.
 Sam followed the sergeant out the door and waited till he yelled orders to one of the guards.

The private escorted Sam and Spotted Fawn to the far end of the fort, where a corral held somewhere around fifty mounts. "Sergeant, said to pick the one you want." He pointed to a smaller corral attached to the side of an adobe tack room. "Those are Injun ponies. No brands... No shoes...Take all of them you want." Sam turned and looked at Spotted Fawn. "Pick you out a pony."

She looked at the ponies and back to Sam. "You pick." Spotted Fawn knew little about the four legged creatures except she did not like to ride them.

The big mountaineer looked over the six horses. "I'll take the paint and that roan over there."

"They're all yourn... You rope em.. I'll hold the gate." The tall skinny army private spat tobacco juice onto the ground between his feet. He reached and removed a rope latch wrapped over the top of the post. .

Sam then threw a loop over the two animals he had picked and led them out onto the parade ground. The private saluted and returned to his post outside the Colonel's office.

Sam and Spotted Fawn walked to a spot the private had pointed out to them between the Sutler's store and another structure. The Sutler was a man hired by the army to purchase and dispense supplies for the soldiers. Although they held the rank of a warrant officer, they had no authority over enlisted men.

There were wet and frightened towns people, cold and shivering from the flooded river, gathered in front of the store as Sam and Fawn passed by, .

Sam found them a spot near the tall outer wall of the fort and they settled in to spend a night. It was the first time they had been alone together since both had committed in their hearts to belong to the other.

Sam took out his Bible and turned to Spotted Fawn... "Do you know this book?"

"I see you read... I see man at mission read. It say you God love everybody." She looked at Sam with curious eyes. "You teach me?"

"I will teach you." Sam opened his Bible and read Romans 3:23 "For all have sinned and fall short of the Glory of God."

"What Glory?" Spotted Fawn still had the curious look on her face.

"Glory is... hmm. Glory is being forgiven for sins by God's grace, I think...No. Glory is the praise and worship we give to God. No, I think Glory is the love of God, the grace, the holiness.... Spotted Fawn... May I just call you Fawn?"

"Yes...I call you Sam!"

"Fawn... I am not a missionary....I am not a priest. I don't know everything in this Book. I don't think man can describe the Glory of God other than He is everywhere" Sam held the Bible up. "I do know there is only one God ... Only one Jesus. Do you know who Jesus is?"

"Missionary say Jesus die for all. That mean me?"

"That means you. That means everybody who believes He died for them. Do you understand?" Sam now had the curious eyes.

"You God... My God. I go with Sam. You teach read book. I stay with Sam."

"I will teach you Fawn. You stay with Sam... We marry. Yes?
"What marry?"
"We go to sleep now. Talk more tomorrow." Sam closed his Bible and lay back onto his arm across the fire from the curious young woman.

——————— ..... ———————

There was noise and lots of activity when Sam and Fawn woke at daylight. Fawn happily started a fire and sat the blue porcelain pot on to boil. She would make Sam the black stuff he liked to drink.
There were people milling around all over the parade ground, soldiers and civilians. The river had risen even higher over the east bank and San Marcial was totally lost.
The one thousand inhabitants of the small town would have to relocate. It would take a while for the few businesses to reestablish themselves in another place. There was already talking of rebuilding on the higher west bank of the Rio Grande.
While spotted Fawn tended the fire, Sam strolled around to the front of the Sutlers store. There were several men exiting the door with bacon and flour on their shoulders. All of them looked angry. When Sam entered behind them he heard the loud booming voice of the big sergeant from yesterday addressing a small wiry man with wire rim glasses on the tip of his nose.

"Mister Jackson! The Colonel sent me with a message for you! You will sell all these people what they need. At army prices! If you run out we will find you more supplies. Do you understand Mister Jackson?!" The sergeant wheeled and started to the door. "Mornin to you, Mister Raines!" Out the door he stomped.
"Good morning Sarge." Sam turned his head and bowed to the sergeant.
"Got any bacon, beans and flour left?" He addressed the frail little man behind the counter.
Mister Jackson found the supplies Sam had requested. "That all?" he asked.
"You have a small canvas tarp and some rope? " Sam asked.
"This do?" he dropped a small canvas cover and a fifty foot length of rope onto the counter.
"That will do." Sam picked up the supplies and walked back around to the where Fawn had prepared coffee for him.
While Fawn cooked a breakfast, Sam picked up all the supplies and packed them on the roan and covered them with the canvas tarp he had brought from the Sutler's store. He made rope harnesses for the roan and the paint.
Fawn would ride the paint alongside Sam and he would trail the pack horse behind them. Fawn watched his every move with anticipation, watching closely as he put the harness on the paint. She brought a slab of cooked bacon wrapped in flat bread over to Sam with a cup of coffee.
"We go now?" Fawn was very uncomfortable, as was Sam, with all the people around.

"We eat, and we go." Sam took a large bite of the food.

——————— ····· ———————

An hour later, Sam and Fawn rode out of the large double gates.

Fawn had managed to straddle the paint pony with a leg up from Sam. She had only ridden twice and both times had been bareback. It was a softer ride for her. The brown and white pony was smaller and gentler than the one Sam rode.

They weaved between wagons full of lumber that was leaving the fort and headed down stream. Civilian drivers were escorted by army troops. They were going to rebuild San Marcial.

Sam and Fawn rode west to go around the large fort then turned north to follow the west bank of the Rio Grande. They could see the raging water rolling down the river, destroying everything in its path on the lower east bank.

When they had cleared the fortress, Sam pulled his New Testament and began to read to Fawn. He started in the first book of John. "In the beginning was the Word…"

They rode slowly for the next three days. Sam read out loud to Fawn as they moved along. Sometimes he would stop and show Fawn words like God and Jesus. In the evening around a fire he tutored her in reading the white man's words from the King James New Testament. They both would laugh when some words were difficult for either of them to pronounce. They were growing close to each other and to the Word of God. Fawn was beginning to see the difference in the wolf god beliefs of the Tonkawa and felt a yearning in her heart to know all she could about the white man's God.

"White man God, my God" she spoke to Sam with conviction one night as they talked through the vows they would make to each other.

On the fourth day away from Fort Craig, they saw a settlement on the west bank of the Rio Grande River. They would arrive in the town by midafternoon. When Sam saw a sign for the township he read it aloud to Fawn so she could see the letters and call out, Socorro.

Sam saw something else as they approached Socorro. A cross rose into the heavens from a tall adobe mission. It was San Miguel Mission De Socorro. It was the Lord calling to them.

Together they felt the Winds of the Rio Grande as they rode along the wild and raging river.

ELEVEN

*For this reason a man shall leave his father and his mother and
be joined to his wife; and they shall become one flesh.
And the man and his wife are both naked and were not ashamed.*
Genesis 2:24-25

Socorro was located on the west bank of the Rio Grande. The elevation of the river was near to five thousand feet, quite different from the end of the Rio Grande to the south of Big Bend.

Fawn was amazed at the difference. She had not seen trees like this before. On her first venture to New Mexico Territory the Tonkawa had not gone this far north.

The Rio Grande was still a raging torrent. Uprooted trees were swirling in the current like huge boats being forced along on the white churning water.

Two Christians rode through the small town of Socorro, focused on the cross at Mission San Miguel that towered above every other building.

The San Miguel Mission was situated on the north edge of the small town. It was encompassed by a huge garden that surrounded it on every side. Flowers that had been planted by Indians in the spring were now in full bloom. Purple sage created a blue fence around the entire property.

The mission sat on a Spanish Land Grant that measured nearly three miles from the center of the sanctuary to the four compass headings of North, South, East, and West.

What a sight for the two young adventurers. Sam had prayed with Fawn the evening before, and she had accepted the Lord Jesus Christ as her Savior. They believed the Lord had led them to this magnificent garden. Fawn remembered the story Sam had told her about Adam and Eve in the Garden of Eden. She would not allow the serpent to tempt her as had Eve. There was a burning desire in her heart to know more.

Red men of several tribes worked in the garden as Sam and Fawn rode onto the grounds. Sam recognized some as Apache. There were Navajo and Pueblo cliff dwellers too.

A cobblestone path led them through the garden amongst stares from curious eyes. They rode as slowly as the horses would take them, sometimes coming to a complete stop to look in awe at the beautiful, colorful blooms that had been created by the Lord.

Sam stared in wonder at the structure in front of them. Nothing in San Antonio, Texas could match this tall mission. Even from a distance you had to crane your neck to see the only windows high up on the walls. The walls alone were five feet thick throughout the whole mission.

Finally they pulled up in front of a massive wooden door and dismounted the horses. Fawn had become adept at jumping on and off the brown and white pony. She loved to ride the animal now, especially alongside Sam as he read to her.

The door to the mission squeaked as it slowly swung open to the inside. A young priest in a brown flowing robe greeted them and flung the hood back from his head.

"Good afternoon my children... Welcome to the house of the Lord... How may I help you?"

Sam's face became as red as Fawns. It was the first time he would have to tell someone else what they were up to.

"We...We want to get married." He stumbled through the words.

The young priest smiled. "Won't you come in." He pushed hard to move the door open. He waved to two red teen agers who were standing nearby as Sam and Fawn entered the huge dark room. The two youths led the three horses away around the building.

Sam removed his floppy hat as they were directed to the rear of a large candlelit room. There were oaken knee pads, lining each side of the center aisle. On one sidewall was a replica of the winged Saint Michael, the arc angel, carrying a large shiny silver Sword. On the back wall, up high, Jesus hung on a cross. It was totally silent as they made their way to a candlelit altar.

"I am Brother Francisco," the young priest spoke and it echoed throughout the room. "Father Sebastian will perform the ceremony. Are you both believers in our Lord, Jesus Christ?"

"Yes… Yes…" Sam stammered. "I was baptized back in Mississippi, in a little creek." He remembered back to when he had accepted Jesus, as a twelve year old boy. He and his friend Benjamin and Benjamin's sister Elizabeth had been submerged into a cold spring fed, Mississippi creek.

"And the young lady?" Brother Francisco was well aware of the red man's beliefs. It had been a struggle to salvage the few souls of those who worked around the mission.

"Spotted Fawn's Christian now!" Beaming the young red woman exclaimed. "Jesus save me. Sam pray for me. I pray."

Sam smiled at Fawns exuberance.

"Spotted Fawn accepted Jesus just last night. She is very proud. We love each other. We will serve the Lord together…As man and wife."

"I will speak to Father Sebastian. First I think he will want to baptize Spotted Fawn. I will get the Father and return shortly. You may wait here." Brother Francisco disappeared through a dark doorway.

Sam and Fawn kneeled at the altar and waited. Just as they began to pray, a figure came rushing through the door that Brother Francisco had gone through. He was a large man like Sam.

"Come… Come, follow me." Father Sebastian was a jovial man, proud to serve his Maker. He strode in large reaching steps to the right side of the sanctuary. His robe was worn and tattered at the back hem from many days of dragging it behind him. When he stopped and turned he was standing in front of a stone pedestal with a large earthen bowl perched on top. There were beads of pure silver running up the four corners of the stone pillar. The silver created a lace basket to hold the bowl in place. On one edge of the bowl was a small embroidered silk handkerchief.
"Come my dear." He waved Spotted Fawn to stand by the baptismal bowl filled with holy water.
Fawn looked at Sam and tentatively approached the priest.
"Who brings this young woman to be baptized?"
Sam looked at Brother Francisco and nodded in the affirmative.
"I do." He spoke nervously.
"Young woman do you accept Jesus as your Lord and Savior?" His booming voice echoed throughout the chamber.
"I Christian. I love Jesus." Fawn spoke softly.
"'Then I baptize you in the name of the Father, the Son and the Holy Ghost!" Father Sebastian sprinkled water onto the forehead of Spotted Fawn with the large rough finger of a working man. He picked up the silk handkerchief and gently wiped her brow.
"Brother Francisco," he boomed. "Make a certificate for this young lady. Now… Who are going to marry?"

Sam was caught off guard. He loved Fawn and wanted very much to spend his life with her. It suddenly was upon him that he was about to become a husband.
Spotted Fawn spoke up. "I marry Sam."
"Yes... yes..., I will marry Spotted Fawn." Sam took a deep breath.

"Brother Francisco, see if you can round up a couple of sisters. We will wait at the altar... Come, come children, can't sleep in the Lord's house together till you are wed."

Sam's mind began racing Sleep...? Together...? In the Lords house...? Now he was really becoming nervous. He heard a door slam behind him, echoing throughout the huge hall. Brother Francisco scurried down the center aisle behind two sisters dressed in black with white head coverings.

"Dearly beloved," Sam turned back as Father Sebastian began the wedding ceremony. He stood trying to understand each word that boomed out of the large jovial man of God. It was all a blur to him and then Father Sebastian was speaking those magic words. "I now pronounce you man and wife. You may kiss the bride."

Neither of the newlyweds had ever kissed anyone before .It was an awkward feeling for both of them. As their lips made contact. Spotted Fawn looked up into Sam's eyes and a broad smile crossed her beautiful young face.

"Sister Maria Martha, find these two newlyweds food and lodging, then leave them alone." Father

Sebastian walked away with a loud happy laugh ringing through the hall.

The newlyweds stayed two full days at San Miguel De Socorro. They spent their days walking about all the beautiful flower gardens and visiting with the many brothers and nuns. On occasion they would run into the jovial priest, Father Sebastian. He was always busy but stopped to bless them each time. In the evenings, they awkwardly became accustomed to being married.

---------- ..... ----------

Early on the third morning Sam and Fawn said their good byes to a place they would never forget. It was July tenth when the two rode northwest out of Socorro and away from the San Miguel mission. They skirted the river and made their way into the foothills of a mountain range. There was still a desert atmosphere even at the higher elevation.

By noon they traveled within sight of Polvadera, another of the small settlements on the west bank of the Rio Grande. Fawn was happy to be riding along listening to her husband read the scripture to her. Husband and wife were new words to her. Adding a last name to Spotted Fawn was strange to her culture. She kept repeating it out loud to Sam.

"Spotted Fawn Raines, Spotted Raines, Fawn Raines. Why I need new name?" She asked.

"It is a custom for the woman in the white man's world to take the name of her husband."

"It is God's way?" She asked him.

"It is God's way." Sam answered.

"Then I am Fawn Raines, wife of Sam Raines." She smiled broadly.

They crossed a smaller river to the north and west of Polvadera. It was not a wild and raging river like the Rio Grande. As the rivers divided, Sam and Fawn followed the smaller quieter water for a way. The Rio Grande was still visible as a fast running torrent east of their trail.

Fawn pulled back on the rope bridle Sam had made for her and leaned forward straining into the distance. Sam stopped reading and looked at the face of his wife, wondering why she had stopped so suddenly. She pointed up the bank of the narrow river. There was a large plume of black smoke rising high into the sky. It was not a campfire but something much larger that burned.

After the incident with the Comancheros the newlyweds proceeded at a slow cautious pace. The fire was an hour away when Fawn had first noticed it.

It was eerily quiet as they drew close to the fire. The smoke began to diminish to a white trickle spiraling upward above the horizon.

Sam was the first to make out what was burning. There were two Conestoga wagons burned down to the axles. The canvas covering and the box that had served as a home to the travelers, who were searching for a new life, were completely burned away.

The pioneers had been caught slowing down to look for a river crossing when they were attacked.

Sam and Fawn warily looked in all directions as they approached the smoldering wagons. There were unshod hoof tracks all around. Two large trunks were opened with clothing scattered all over the place. The horses that had drawn the wagons were gone.

Fawn touched Sam's shoulder and pointed between one of the sets of wheels. An arm was visible on the ground near one of the wheels. Sam looked around again then dismounted, handing Fawn the end of his bridle. He slowly raised his Sharps and walked around between the two wagons, stepping gingerly over the broken wagon tongue.

There were four bodies stacked in a pile alongside the lead wagon. Two were white males and two were women. All four had been shot with arrows. Sam could see by the dripping blood they had been stacked one on the other then all were scalped. One of the women was with a child.

Sam walked to the pack animal and removed a shovel. With tears streaming down his face he dug a grave in the hot desert sand. Fawn brought a canteen to her husband and stood alongside as he read over the grave from his Bible. When he had finished she picked an arrow up from the ground. "Pache!" She threw the arrow back onto the desert sand.

While Sam fashioned a crude cross of wagon flooring for the grave Fawn walked down along the river bank where one the trunks had been turned on its side. There were two things she did not expect to see. The first was clothing scattered about on the sand. Among them she saw children's garments. The second was footprints leading into the river. Two sets of footprints. They were too small to be one of the four victims Sam had buried.

"Sam!" She called. "Sam... Come see!"

Sam tapped the top of the cross one last time with the back of the shovel and walked to where Fawn stood on the river bank. She did not speak, but pointed to the clothes and then to the footprints.

Sam's eyes followed the two sets of tracks into the river and onto the other bank. He saw where two young people had stumbled to their knees in a rush to get out of the river. Twenty yards from the opposite side of the narrow waters, Sam saw a cluster of large boulders surrounded by Yucca and Sage. The tracks stopped there. Sam looked at Fawn. "Those are children. They must have watched what happened here. We have to go get them."

Fawn was first to be mounted and waited for Sam. They rode slowly across the river and toward the boulders, not wanting to panic the children. As they approached the hiding place two children bolted and ran out into the desert. One of them was a boy of about twelve, the other a girl, nine or ten years old.

Sam spurred his mount and rode swiftly after the boy scooping him up into his arms. Fawn jumped from the paint and caught the girl. Both of the children began kicking and screaming as they were lifted off the ground. The newlyweds held the young ones tightly to their breast until the kicking and screaming abated into uncontrollable sobbing.

Winds of the Rio Grande

TWELVE

If a brother sister is without clothing and in need of daily food, and one of you says to them, "Go in peace, be warmed and be filled," and yet you do not give them what is necessary for their body, what is that? James 2:15-16

Sam and Fawn walked back across the river holding the youngsters in their arms and leading the horses behind them. Gathering what few clothes were left for them, Sam lifted the boy onto the pack horse and the girl up behind Fawn on the paint. They took the two young orphans away from the scene of the massacre to a spot on the bank of the Rio Grande. Fawn started a fire and put a pot of coffee on to boil. She cut bacon into strips and dropped them into a hot frying pan, then rolled out flat bread and laid it on hot rocks to warm through. The two children sat across the fire huddled closely together. They watched every move that Fawn made as she busily moved around the fire.

Sam hobbled the horses near the river and came back to the fire.

"I'm Sam... This is my wife Fawn, What are your names?"

The two children huddled closer together unsure of what to do. The boy spoke,

"Is...Is she an Injun!" He pointed to Fawn.

"Yes she is. She is not Apache like those who attacked you're..." Sam let the words trail off. "She is Tonkawa, a friendly tribe. She is my wife."

"She's a redskin... I don't like redskins. "They killed our Ma and Pa." The boy was showing rage in his voice

"Fawn did not hurt your Ma and Pa. She is not like Apache." Sam reiterated.

"Ry... Ry," The little girl pulled at her brother's sleeve. "I'm hungry Ry."

The boy watched the bacon sizzling in the pan. "Can we have something to eat?" He looked at Sam.

"Ask the cook." Sam turned to Fawn. "What do you think cook? Got anything for these two to eat?"

Fawn wrapped bacon in two pieces of bread, stood and walked to the two frightened, starving children. At first they cowered away, the boy glaring at her with hate in his eyes, and then tentatively reached out for the food. Sam laid a canteen close enough for the boy to reach.

"Ry... Is that your name?" He asked again.

"Ryan, my name is Ryan. My sister's name is Sissy... Melissa, but we call her Sissy, Can we have some more?" He pointed to the fry pan.

"Sure." Sam looked at Fawn who was already wrapping bread around bacon.

The boy picked up the canteen, opened it and passed it to Sissy.

"What is your last name Ryan?"

"Hale." He took another bite. "Our name is Hale." After taking a long drink from the canteen he asked", Where you taking us?"

"Where do you want to go? Got any kin around here?" Sam tried to gently pull information out of the boy.

"Got no kin... Ceptin our Ma and Pa back there..." Tears welled up in his eyes.

"Uncle Charles and Aunt Ginny... They back there too, they our only other kin."

Sam and Fawn exchanged glances. "Where did you come from?"

"Tennessee. Knoxville, Tennessee. We going to Californy. My daddy and Uncle Charles fought in the war."

"Would you like for us to take you somewhere you can find a way to Californy?"

"Yes sir, we want to go to Californy like Pa said."

Sam took out his New Testament and moved closer to the fire so he could see the pages. Fawn brought the two youngsters a blanket, then quietly retreated and sat next to her husband.

The mountain man read softly to Fawn until the two young ones went to sleep wrapped tightly in each other arms. Sam and Fawn prayed for them. They also went to sleep, wrapped in each other arms.

When Sam woke at the first light, Fawn was setting the porcelain pot on the fire. The brother and sister sat huddled in the blanket keeping a close eye on Fawn. It didn't matter that she had given them the blanket to sleep in and fed them. She was still an Injun.

The Rio Grande had lost part of its roar from the snow that cascaded down from the mountains. It now was settling back into its banks. The water coming down was still clear and cold from the snow covered mountains of Colorado.

Sam and Fawn were both deeply concerned about the young orphans, and wondered what was to become of them. The prospect of a half grown family was well beyond the feelings of the young newlyweds.

"Did your pa have any money left?" Sam had not looked around the wagons.

"No sir. Him and Uncle Charles used all they had to buy the wagons and horses. Why? Ryan Hale looked at Sam suspiciously"

"Where did they buy the wagons?"

"Back in Oklahoma. I don't remember the town. Pa and Uncle Charles worked some in Alb... Albuquerque... I think that's how you say it. They worked in a livery for a month... I mucked out stables, just got nough to buy food for the trip to Calforny. No money left...." Tears began streaming down the boy's face.

"Ok son.... That's alright. No need to fret. You don't need money. You know anybody in Albuquerque?"

"Just the Preacher and Miss Ruth, That's his wife." Ryan Hale was having a hard time talking through the choked back sobs. He wanted to be strong for Sissy, but missed their Ma and Pa something terrible.

He had to try to be strong, because he was the only man left in the family.

"Sissy, do you know the preacher?" Sam tried to relieve some of the pressure from Ryan.

"Yes sir.... It was preacher McKin... McKin..." Sissy looked up to her brother Ryan.

"It was preacher McKinley!" Ryan blurted out the name. "First name of Joseph. He baptized me and Sissy. He dunked us in the river."

"It was cold too!" Sissy spoke out.

"Do you want to go back to Albuquerque? See the preacher?"

"Yes sir. I guess so. We got nowhere else to go. Ok by you Sissy?" Ryan wiped his eyes and runny nose on his shirt sleeve.

"Uh huh." was Sissy's only response.

———— ... ————

Fawn's mind was not on the words that Sam read to her as they moved along the trail. She had never had anyone be afraid of her. Her heart went out to the two young white children. Their parents had been brutally murdered by someone of her color. The white race tended to lump all people with red skin into one murderous band of savages. What was her life going to be like in the white man's world of her husband?

"Miss Fawn." Sissy was riding behind her on the paint. "Are all red man's bad?"

Fawn didn't know how to answer.

"No, all red men are not bad." Sam broke in. "Just like all white men are not good. One of the best men I've ever known was a red man called Castile. He was Miss Fawn's uncle and my best friend."

"Why did them red men kill our Ma and Pa?" Ryan asked the question this time.

"They were Apache." Sam explained. "They are a warring Nation, who hates white men. The whites killed a lot of their women and children. Don't go through your life hating a man for the color of his skin."

No one spoke for a long while. Fawn was very proud of Sam for what he had said.

As long as they stayed close to the river they could see for miles in all directions. After the attack by Apaches on the Hale family, Sam and Fawn were even more wary of their surroundings.

The sun was sinking low in the western sky as they found a place on the river bank to make camp. Sam walked out into the dusk, gazing into a yellow and orange panoramic sunset.

The mountain between him and the beautiful sky had a bright red glow. Gray and black clouds moved serenely over the peaks, seeming to float across the sky.

Sam removed the knife from his scabbard and chopped off eight of the purple red cactus pears from flat padded Napals. Cutting one of the Napal pads, he used it for a plate for carrying the pears back to the fire. It would be a treat for the orphans and they all would have Napolito for breakfast.

Fawn smiled when Sam sat the treats near the fire she had started. She peeled the pears and warmed them next to the fire before passing them to the youngster. They had never had the pulpy fruit of cactus pears, and thoroughly enjoyed the treat.

Three days later the four travelers saw the city of Albuquerque rising out of the north eastern sky.

The one structure that showed above all the others was a somewhat familiar sight to Sam and Fawn. The San Felipe de Neri Mission overwhelmed the skyline of Albuquerque.

The city was spread along both banks of the Rio Grande River, sprawling for miles on either side with a mixture of cultures and races. There were nearly ninety thousand people scattered throughout the bustling community that was divided down the middle by the Rio Grande.

Sam and Fawn had never seen so many people in one place. Both of them were at times in awe of all the activities, and at times very uneasy in these surrounding. The two youngsters had been here before, but were frightened to be without their Ma and Pa for protection.

Sam and Fawn knew from their previous experience that there would be help at the mission. They rode through the dusty streets in the direction of the twin steeples. Loud piano music and raucous laughter filled the streets through swinging saloon doors. People of all races and colors intertwined, sharing in the drinking and carousing on and off the streets.

Fawn nudged the paint to draw nearer to Sam. Sissy buried her head into the red woman's back and squeezed tightly with her hands together around her waist. Ryan closed his eyes and held on to the canvas tarp covering the supplies.

Sam kept his gaze straight ahead except for the occasional look to the sky to search out the steeples. He did not want to provoke any of the rowdy people they encountered along the way.

Finally, they turned a corner and the entrance to the large church loomed into view. Like the San Miguel Mission in Socorro the San Felipe De Neri was surrounded by a beautiful garden of trees and flowers. The five foot thick walls were also the same as the San Miguel Mission.

To one side of the huge entrance two men in brown robes were standing immersed in conversation. The younger man saw them coming and, touching the other man on the shoulder, pointed in their direction. The older priest turned to welcome them.

"Accueillir" the priest spoke in a language Sam had never heard.

He replied to him in English "Father?"

"Parlez-vous le francais?"

"Sir?" Sam was confused.

The other Priest spoke in the foreign language to the father, then addressed Sam in English.

"Father is French. He is Father Jean Baptiste Labonte. I am Brother Antoine. I am also French, but I have been here longer and have learned your language."

"We are looking for a Baptist Minister name of Joseph McKinley. Can you help us?" Sam spoke to the brother, relieved that he spoke in his language

"I think so," he spoke to the other father in French.

The father answered, "Montrez la voie a thhem, la frère. Oui?'

The French priest was not like the large jovial man who had married Sam and Fawn. He was a tall, slender, younger man with black curly hair.

"I will show you," The brother smiled at Sam." I hope you can still find him. We heard he and his wife were going to Santa Fe. He doesn't have a church in Albuquerque. He mostly talks to people on the streets

Brother Antoine pointed north along the Rio Grande and told Sam where to find the protestant preacher.

The little caravan rode out the north cobblestone walk and along the river bank. They had moved beyond the limits of Albuquerque and continued for another half mile.

A small wagon loaded with a piano and a small table with two chairs was stopped near the river. Two horses were staked out in a small patch of grass. A man and woman sat on the ground adjacent to a small fire. Both got to their feet as the riders approached.

"Howdy brother... Mam." The tall lean man greeted them.

"Howdy," Sam responded. "We're looking for Reverend McKinley. Is that you?"

"Yes, it is brother. This is my wife Ruth." He spotted the boy on the pack horse. "Ryan... Is that you boy? Where's your Ma and Pa?"

"I'm Sam Raines, Reverend." Sam reached down and put out his hand, intentionally interrupting the preacher. "This is my wife Fawn... We found Ryan and Sissy in the desert." Sam dismounted and approached the couple. "Their Ma and Pa were killed by Apaches." He lowered his voice.

"On my Lord!" The reverend's wife spoke for the first time. She rushed to Fawns horse and took Sissy down from behind the red woman. She held the young girl close to her chest and tears began streaming down her face.

"They wanted to come to you Reverend. Didn't know where else to bring them." Sam informed the minister of the children's desire.

"Why don't you all get down, just have a pot of beans and cornpone, but you're welcome" Ruth McKinley invited them to share their food.

Sam and Fawn dismounted, and the two of them helped Ryan down from the pack animal. They walked together to the fire. Neither Ryan nor Sissy had yet spoken.

"You leaving Albuquerque Reverend?" Sam had noticed the wagon and their direction out of town and put it together with what the brother had said...

"Sam... I didn't get your last name, Sam."

"It's Raines… Samson and Spotted Fawn Raines. We got married by the priest in Socorro."

"Well…. Congratulations! Glad to know you got married in one of God's churches." The minister was truly elated. "To answer your question, Mister Raines, I've been mostly a circuit preacher since the Lord called me to serve him some ten years ago. Santa Fe has offered to build us a church, Ruth and Me."

Ruth chimed in, "Going to live in a real house right next to our new church."

"What about these children?" Sam looked at Fawn and back to the Pastor's wife.

"Why we will take them with us, won't we Joseph?" Ruth spoke again emphatically.

"Yes, we will my dear." Pastor McKinley replied. "That okay with you children?"

Ryan and Sissy both shook their heads yes.

The pastor got to his feet. "Let us pray for these children" All four adults stood and encircled the two young Hale children. All four of them lifted prayers of thanks to the heavens. Sam and Fawn were confident that the McKinley's would take good care of the two orphans.

THIRTEEN

The Lord is my shepherd, I shall not want.
He makes me lie down in green pastures; He leads me beside
quiet waters.
He restores my soul; He guides me in the paths of righteousness
For His name sake.
Psalms 23; 1-3

Sam and Fawn traveled along with Pastor Joseph McKinley and Ruth for another day until they reached the turnoff that took the wagon and the new family to a home in Santa Fe.

The mountain man and his wife dismounted and said their farewells to the children they had rescued from a sure death only days before. They had formed a bond that would be with them all for years to come. It was with strong emotion that they left the two Hale children.

When they had departed their new friends, Sam passed the New Testament to Fawn and spurred his horse away. Fawn pulled back on the rope reins and sat for a moment staring at her husband's back.

The Winds of the Rio Grande flipped the pages of the Bible and stopped at the book of James. Slowly she began to read. 'James, a bond servant of God and of the Lord Jesus Christ, To the twelve tribes who are dispersed abroad; Greetings. Consider it all joy, my brethren, when you encounter various trials, knowing that the testing of your faith produces endurance.' She clucked her horse and again looked down at the words on the page. Sam had faith that she was ready to read the words without his help.

Riding at a leisurely pace that day they missed the youngsters, but also were glad to be alone again to continue the love they had found in each other.

At dusk the terrain was beginning to drastically change from the river they had traveled.

Sam's heart felt a pang of relief as they began to see trees that he had only seen in the Chisos Mountains in South Texas Big Bend Country. The earth was rising up on both sides of the river creating a great gorge for the waters to flow through. The sky was bright orange engulfing the entire horizon. Black clouds floated lazily above the deep canyon. Cap rock rose and fell as the elevation changed. There were high pointed peaks and flat mesas that seemed to run for miles.

Sam and Fawn both sat astride their horses gaping with eyes wide and mouths open at what lay beyond them. Neither of them had ever seen such glorious splendor in the world that God had created. They watched as the sun crept over the mountain tops on the western horizon. The Rio Grande River had an eerie but serene glow as it trickled white water over rocks in mid-stream and cascaded out of the huge cavern. The rocks were another indication that Sam was about to be in the environment that he loved. He was getting closer to the great Rocky Mountains.

He took a breath of fresh clean air and slowly lifted his right leg over the horse and stepped down. Fawn brought her right leg over the horse's neck and slid quietly to the ground. Neither spoke as Sam gathered firewood from under the spruce umbrellas that would cover them this night.

As Sam enjoyed a hot cup of coffee, Fawn read the words to him that she had felt in her heart earlier.

They slept soundly cuddled in each other's arms as two of God's children who loved each other deeply.

Fawn was the first awake as was her normal routine. She stoked the fire and added dry fir limbs. She casually stood and walked to the river's edge to wash her face in the cold clear water. Sam was rising as she walked past him, and the fire, smiling at him.

She was on her way to retrieve the bacon and flour from the pack animal, when she suddenly realized the quietness of the moment. Then she grasped what was wrong.

"Sam…Sam!" She looked around then turned to Sam who was washing in the river. "Sam… The horses! The horses gone!"

Sam jumped to his feet and ran quickly to her side. "They must have broken loose and wandered off. I'll go look for them." He walked to the spot where he had staked the animals, looking for hoof prints to trail.

After a minute he picked up a trail. The horses were moving back down the river from where they came. "I'll go see." He started off.

"I come too, I see footprints too." Fawn looked at him with fear on her face.

Sam had seen several footprints made by moccasins. He didn't know Fawn had seen them, too. They were leading the horses downstream. They weren't trying to hide their tracks. The two of them together trailed the horse thieves down the river for a mile until the tracks disappeared into thin air.

There was no need to go further so they backtracked to their camp sight, looking for other tracks along the way. Whoever had taken their mounts was very quiet, and the newlyweds had slept very deeply and peacefully.

Reality sat in as they looked up the river into the deep gorge. They were alone in a wilderness that neither knew anything about. They had choices to make. Did they go back down the Rio Grande to Santa Fe or Albuquerque? Neither of them wanted to be in a civilized world with all those people.

Sam spoke first. "I didn't come all this way to give up and go back. Do you want to go back to the Tonkawa...To your people?"

"Sam Raines my people! Go where Sam go. I your wife!" She looked again at the deep chasm in front of them. "We go top of ridge or down in?"

"I can see places along the bank to camp." They both took a long look into the gorge. "I don't know how long the canyon is, but there is water... I don't know about up top."

Sam knew they must have water to survive. He also knew that Fawn knew the ways of the wild and how to find food. From up where they were, he could also see white water rapids separated by long calm, peaceful pools of still water. There must be fish.

Sam and Fawn sat on rocks opposite, facing each other. They held hands and bowed in prayer. They were happy the Lord was with them. They stood together and began slowly picking their way over the rocks and descending into a land, they did not know. It was slow going down the steep incline. The beginning of the gorge was made up of rolling hills that tumbled down to the river's edge and it was difficult to stay upright as they made their way down. They were becoming even more aware of their surroundings after the loss of their horses and supplies. It dawned on Sam that he had also lost his Sharps rifle. The only weapons left for survival were the revolver at his side and a knife in a scabbard attached to the back of his gun belt.

Fawn was more used to walking in all kinds of terrain than Sam. She stepped out into the lead. It took them more than two hours to reach the river bank. Both kneeled at the water's edge and drank from the clear cold stream, before proceeding up the river and through the gorge.

They checked around for footprints. Although they saw none, both were aware that Indians were very good at covering their tracks.

They moved very slowly and cautiously that first day and were just beginning to make it into the steep walls of the gorge and the sun went behind the west wall earlier than it did out in open country. They found the air to be much cooler down in the deep crevice. One thing they found on the first day was that they must collect firewood where they found it along the way.

They had been in and out of the water all day. Sometimes the banks of the river were up against the high walls on both sides with nowhere to walk, but in the water. At other times there were flats or ledges to make their way on. Occasionally they found small sand or lava bars that acted like an oasis. There was little conversation that first day, but both realized that at the pace they were forced to go this was going to be a long, long journey.

Sunlight was off and on and not for very long. Walking in and out of the water in a perpetual shade made their bodies cold, even in the hot July weather.

They came upon a sandy island and crawled out of the water to build a small fire and warm their bodies. Most of the warmth on that first night would come from snuggling close and creating body heat.

There was no wood for a morning fire and no food to warm their bellies as they began another day.

By the end of July they had made only a short distance through the steep canyon. Their bodies were bruised and battered from bouncing back and forth on jagged rocks while traversing white water rapids.

The food was sparse. Mostly they had eaten fish. Sometimes raw and if they were lucky enough to stumble onto enough wood for a fire they had warm broiled fish to warm their innards. Those days were few. Once Sam had killed a snake and skinned it. They ate it raw.

It was beginning to become harder for both of them to navigate. They were getting weak from the lack of food and tired from the struggles of maintaining their movement along the cold river waters. Both of them had fallen many times and were cut and scratched over their entire bodies.

It was into the first week of August when the two torn and tattered travelers came around a bend in the canyon river and saw yet another set of rapids to maneuver.

It was about one hundred yards through the roaring white waters.

The sun was straight overhead and it was near noon as they struggled into the rushing water. The pressure on their legs made it hard to place one leg in front of the other. At times Sam put Fawn on his back and carried her through stretches where there were no rocks to hold onto. Sometimes they were knocked off their feet, giving some of the distance they had traversed, back to the river. They silently pulled themselves back to their feet and continued upward.

Sam had stopped to reach out and help Fawn through two slippery rocks when he looked up the river. Thirty yards away was the beginning of another long pool of still water. This one was different. Jutting from the lava sidewall of the canyon were three large pine trees. There would be firewood for warmth, and maybe a soft bundle of needles to lie on. He touched Fawn on the shoulder and pointed. It gave both of them the incentive they needed to finish the struggle for another thirty yards.

Sam lifted Fawn with his last bit of strength and sat her out of the cold water onto the sunny bar. It was the first time in days they had felt heat penetrating their bodies. It felt so good.

When Sam had dragged himself onto the warm sand, the two of them wrapped in each other's arms. They gave praise to God for where He had brought them this day. From sheer exhaustion they slept. Their clothes had dried in the heat of God's sun and both slept the entire night.

When they woke there was a new freshness to the air and warmth again when the sun peaked over the canyon wall. It felt good to be alive. Sam immediately gathered dried sticks and needles from beneath the three jutting pine trees. With his knife and flint he turned a small spark into a roaring blaze. He removed the New Testament from his waist band and laid it in the bright sunlight to dry.

Fawn was back in the water in a pool just above the rapids. When Sam looked she was already tossing a second colorful trout onto the bank. Fish for breakfast! He smiled at his wife.

For the first time in almost a month, the Word of God was dried out enough to turn the pages and read. Sam laid his head back onto a stack of soft pine needles and listened as Fawn read haltingly to him from the Bible. He closed his eyes and absorbed all that she read.

This was a time of healing and restoration. The young married couple spent a week in God's warm Garden of Eden. When their bodies had recovered and they had eaten enough fish to replenish themselves, they knew they must move along again. They did not know how much further the gorge would hold them hostage.

They had only gone two bends up the river when they encountered another set of roaring white water.

FOURTEEN

Even though I walk through the valley of the shadow of death, I will fear no evil, for You are with me; Your rod and Your staff, they comfort me. Psalm 23:4

Forty days later two gaunt and starving people looked up from a cold running Rio Grande River. In the not distant sky to the north they saw something different. Instead of the tall black lava walls of the gorge, they saw rolling hills and above them white cumulous clouds floated across a bright blue sky.

Another forty days after their respite, God had given them the answer to their prayer. They were one day from climbing out of the Rio Grande Gorge.

It was late September and in the northern New **Mexico Territory the long hot summer was coming to** an end. A chill in the air meant an early fall was coming to the Rocky Mountains. Sam and Fawn had experienced the cold fall air all summer as they made their way through the great gorge. Very slowly the pair climbed out of the deep valley and into the rolling hills. They were weak and hungry and lacked the strength and energy to climb the rocky terrain. They tried to stay on their feet but continuously slipped and fell onto their knees. Their moccasins were long gone. The small sharp rocks had made it hard to stay erect and walk on bare, cut and bruised feet. They crawled over the rocks until their knees hurt so badly they would fall onto their side and lie until the pain abated, then move slowly along once more.

---------- ….. ----------

The Ute Mountain Ute Indians were a nomadic tribe who traveled mostly within their own territory. The mountain was their god Manitou. In the late winter months when snow covered the passes they left the mountain in search of food in the lower elevations. Food was what generally dictated their reason for travels. Most of their food supply was derived from plants and berries or animals and fish they found in the valleys and streams. They dried food to get them through the long cold mountain winters. They were a tribe that was hungry a lot in cold weather.

They spread into family groups to search for enough to feed the smaller numbers of mouths. The grandfather of each family unit, including aunts and uncles, decided when it was time to move on.

One of the Ute families was on the move to get back to Manitou before the white blanket of the changing season covered them. They had had a good spring and the tribe had gathered in early June for the annual Bear dance before separating again into smaller units to look for food. It had been a productive summer and they were packing many horses loaded with dried buffalo, rabbits, deer and other game that was smoked to feed them through the long cold weather.

It was a small caravan consisting of twelve adults riding along in single file, each towing behind two pack animals with food. The younger adult members were responsible for keeping a remuda of horses that were a treasure of the family.

Since the Spaniards had introduced horses into the Native American culture, the Utes had become proficient at stealing horses from other tribes. They were very proud of their strings of ponies.

The teens and young children walked alongside or hitched rides on the pack horses.

A teenage girl, who was wide to the side of the procession, was looking down a hillside toward the Rio Grande River. She stopped short and gazed for a moment at something that had caught her eye. At first she thought it was an animal of some kind. Maybe it was a grizzly cub. Then she realized that what she saw was a red woman lying on the rocky hillside with another person close by her side.

She yelled and waved to her parents who were riding in the caravan. After much discussion, three of the men rode in her direction. Two of them dismounted and handed the third younger warrior their reins.

———————— ….. ————————

Fawn opened her eyes as a shadow made its way across her face, blocking out the bright light. She could make out two black silhouettes between her and the sun. One of the figures knelt at her side and opened a water skin and wet her lips. She sat up grabbing the skin between her hands and tried to suck the cool liquid into her mouth.

She could hear a conversation between several voices. Her head was spinning from the heat and lack of food in her belly. At times her mind cleared and she recognized some of the words she heard. It was not English. Nor was it her tongue of Tonkawa. It was a dialect of the Shoshone that was spoken by many of the plains tribes

She had learned the language when the Tonkawa were driven into the New Mexico territory by the Apache.

Cheyenne, Pueblo, and Utes were just a few who communicated in the words of the Shoshone.

"Sam?" She spoke through dry, parched lips. "Sam?"

"Fawn. Are you alright?" Sam asked in a hoarse raspy voice.

The two of them felt someone pulling and pushing them. Both of them were loaded onto the top of pack animals. Their clothes were torn and shredded and their feet were cut and bleeding. Sam had lost his hat and Fawns braids had long since come apart.

The soft covering on the pack horses was the softest things either of them had felt in months. The slow rolling motion of the horses gait rocked them to sleep

Neither one remembered being taken from the horse's backs. They slept as they had not done for more than forty days since their time on the pine covered sandbar.

Sam was the first to wake. He was in a teepee that was covered with buffalo robes. Trying to get to his feet, he found he could not. His entire body was a shambles, especially his feet. Where is Fawn? He looked around the darkened room for his wife. She was not there. Once more he tried to rise and fell back in excruciating pain.

Three braves came into the teepee and carried him bodily to one of the pack animals. They half lifted, and half threw him, depositing him onto the soft covering. Before he passed out he saw Fawn lying on another of the pack horses.

Four women had quickly dismantled the teepee where he had slept.

He and Fawn both slept through another day. Their minds were clearing somewhat and pangs of hunger were gnawing at their bellies.

They were still separated but this time a woman and two young girls came to each teepee and bathed their feet in some kind of warm, soothing poultice. One of the girls spooned a thick concoction into their mouths. It was some kind of soup with meat and bitter berries.

The following morning they were forced to repeat the events of the day before.

After a week of the same treatment, Fawn came into Sam's teepee followed by an elderly red man and two young braves. The older man reminded Sam of Fawn's grandfather Walks Like a Coyote. One of the braves dropped buckskin trousers and a beaded shirt onto the ground in front of him. The other one threw down a pair of moccasins

He yelled at Sam. "Tee-a-poo-ah....Moonse-patts!"

Fawn smiled and spoke to her husband for the first time in a week. "He said buckskins and moccasins."

The brave spoke loudly again. Pe-ah- namp-butts.'

Fawn laughed. "He say you have big feet."

The older man spoke softly. "N-a-unt?"

Fawn answered and then turned to her husband. "He asked your name."

The flap swung open and the woman who had washed their feet, followed by the same two girls entered.

The woman spoke. "Tav-vash-op-ti....Pan-nah." She placed bowls of dried buffalo jerky and pan bread in front of the three men.

The woman sat for a while as the men chewed the meat and bread. She turned to Fawn. "Soos-pe –ah? Pew-arr-e?"

Fawn smiled and shook her head up and down.

The woman spoke to the old man and all of them quickly got up and left the teepee.

Sam and Fawn were finally alone. He turned to her and asked. "What did she say?"

She asked if we one heart. If we married."

"How do you know their language?"

They are Ute from the mountain Ute. Speak Shoshone like many tribes. I learn some of it many moons ago."

"Are they friendly?' Sam asked

"Friendly to Tonkawa. Not to white man. You marry Tonkawa! You okay. They believe Ute Mountain Manitou. He their god. He throw leaves up…leaves fly away…they birds. The Grizzly Bear ….judge all animals. Utes do bear dance in summer. They go mountain now for winter. Like me and you."

Without another word Fawn left the teepee and returned shortly with a large urn filled with hot water. She gently washed her husband's feet and body. When he had dried he dressed in his new buckskin clothes and moccasins. His feet were still scarred and painful but he could stand and walk, though gingerly at first.

The Raines family sat and talked late into the night. They spent part of the cool, late September evening trying to remember what happened on the forty days in the gorge, and part being grateful that they could not remember. They thanked the Lord for what he had done for them and then they curled up and went to sleep.

The couple woke early to hear the hubbub of a village preparing to move out. The smells of smoke and food filled the brittle morning air. Sam and Fawn were glad to be alive.

Something deep within Sam began to pull at him and bring on the urge to be on the trail to the Colorado Territory. They were so close and yet on foot it would be difficult to reach their destination .The head waters of the Rio Grande seemed so far away.

There was a crisp feel of fall in the air as they raised the flap and stepped into the day.

The old one, Red Eagle, greeted them when he saw them exit the teepee. "Ann-karr Quan--it-ige." Fawn acknowledged the grandfather.

"He is Red Eagle." She said to Sam.

"Cov-vah." The Indian leader turned and pointed to the remuda, then pointed his finger to Sam's chest. :An-karr Nag-gitts."
He smiled at Fawn. "Si-karr."

One of the horse tenders came out of the remuda, leading four horses. One of them was a big Bay stallion the old one had given Sam. The pinto he gave to Fawn. The other two were pack horses already loaded with food and buffalo robes for the two of them.

"For us?" Sam asked in awe and disbelief. "Man-noon-e." He answered.

Sam looked at Fawn who repeated the answer to his question. "All of them." She smiled broadly.

"Pi-equay… Ter-she-ung-gi…. Shan-ee-ch-pi-quay." The old one pointed north then turned and walked away.

"He say, we go at daylight. He say, we go slowly."

The couple spent the rest of the day .visiting around the Ute clan who had become their extended family.

At daybreak the two travelers mounted up to once more begin their journey up the Rio Grande River.

The Ute woman who had taken care of them smiled at Fawn. She moved her hands in a circular motion around her stomach. "Sow-er."

Sam's head swiveled to look at Fawn who smiled back at the woman

"Neg-tig-a-gand….Friend." She giggled and clucked her horse along.

FIFTEEN

"They will call peoples to the mountain; There they will offer righteous sacrifices; For they will draw out the abundance of the seas, and the hidden treasures of the sand." Deuteronomy 33:19

A flurry of light snow was blowing across the surface of the Rio Grande that created urgency in Sam to get on the trail. The wind orbited around the lower elevations of Ute Mountain as they followed the river around it to the west. They were very near to crossing into the Colorado Territory that Sam had longed to find,

Sam stopped his horse and turned to watch their Ute friends turn away from the river to begin a slow ascent to their winter home. The swirling white powder between them soon made it difficult to see the small caravan. As he turned back to the trail, he looked at Fawn to make sure she was riding the new pony okay.

Fawn was massaging her stomach with one hand as she rode along. She smiled at Sam and whispered to herself the word her Ute friend hat uttered. "Sow-er… big belly"

The snow did not last long and only left a light dusting in the grass along the river's edge. It was too early for a sticking white blanket at the lower elevations

They rode along slowly following the winding trail of the river. There were no markers but Sam felt it in his heart when they crossed into the Colorado Territory. He stopped and let Fawn pull alongside him. They both looked to the west and saw the snowcapped mountains called the San Juan. Sam let the words roll softly off his tongue.

"San Juan… Saint John." He smiled at his beautiful young wife. "Home," he pointed to the white, snow covered mountain top.

The terrain along the Rio Grande had not changed much since they climbed out of the gorge. The river was below them in a canyon, but very shallow compared to the nine hundred foot walls that had kept them hostage for so long.

Sam felt a yearning for a hot cup of black coffee when they made camp for the night. He had not had a cup since they were at the southern edge of the gorge, many days ago. He would not have coffee this day either.

They dismounted in an arroyo that was created many years ago by run off into the river many years ago. There was a forty foot drop to the water, but the ravine gave them protection from the wind.

Fawn untied the rawhide straps from the first pack horse and found heavy buffalo robes for her and Sam. There were leggings made from buffalo hides to cover their legs and feet. She even found a floppy buckskin hat. She almost had to jump to put it on Sam's head. The two of them laughed at her futile attempt.

Sam wrapped his arms around Fawn and pulled her closer to him. Something felt different about his wife. He had lost weight and looked gaunt after their ordeal in the gorge. Fawn had too, but after two weeks with the Utes, she was filling out much quicker than he.

Fawn looked into the big man's eyes, "Sow-er." She giggled.

"What is sow-er?" Sam had heard that word before.

Fawns look went from smiles to being very serious. She took Sam's hand and held it to her belly. "Papoose." She said quietly.

"Papoose!" Sam jerked his hand away. "Papoose?"

"We have Papoose." She did not know how to take her husband's reaction.

"Papoose?....When? How?" He was flabbergasted.

"Not know how?" Fawn smiled.

"When....? When Papoose come?"

He had to find a place to make a home. They would have to slow down.

Sam began to watch every move that Fawn made. She was carrying a child in her belly. He did not want her to harm herself or the baby. "Baby," He had never heard the word in reference to himself. "Daddy," He was going to be a daddy.

"Papoose come when first flower bloom." Fawn brought him back to the present. "Many moons. Plenty time to get to mountain. We build log house, then wait."

"I build log house… You wait!" Sam didn't want Fawn lifting and working. He would take care of her.

Three days after Sam knew they were going to be parents, a large strange valley opened before them. It looked as if they were entering a great desert with huge sand dunes like they had never seen. It was an awesome sight. Some of the shifting dunes rose as high as seven hundred feet. The Rio Grande weaved its way for more than a hundred miles through this incredible desert. This desert was unlike any other. Lakes were nestled all through the valley among the dunes.

Most deserts had hard to find waterholes that people had lost their lives in search of. There would be no shortage of water in this valley.

The second day into the San Luis valley, the wind suddenly increased across the dunes from the southwest. It very quickly became a stinging, blinding sand storm. Sam stepped from his mount and made sure all of the animals were tied securely together. He stayed on foot and led the short train through the tornado like winds. He stumbled along blindly into the storm. He pulled his hat down to cover his eyes but the sand had already done the damage. Sam could not see where he was going or what lay ahead of them. He struggled to find his way and not being able to see, tumbled head first down one of the dunes, but had a tight hold on the horses' reins, pulling them down with him.

All at once they were sheltered from the wind by a vertical wall of brown sand. Sam heard a thud as something fell hard onto the sand behind him.

"Fawn! Fawn….!" He ripped his hat away and thrashed about trying to find his wife through the burning grit that filled his eyes, blinding him. He dropped to his knees and crawled around reaching out with one hand.

"Sam… Sam… I ok. I get off horse then fall." Fawn pulled the buffalo robe away from her face and saw Sam crawling toward her on his hands and knees in the sand. She reached out and touched his extended hand.

Sam recoiled quickly, and then realized it was Fawn that had touched him. "Are you sure you're okay? What about the Baby? Can you see the horses? We need to take care of the horses."

"Papoose ok…. Maybe need food." Fawn laughed. She looked around and found they had fallen into a cavern that was created with walls on three sides by the shifting desert sand. She pulled the horses into the shelter and found a canteen to wash the sand from Sam's eyes. She had managed to get her eyes covered before the sand permeated them. Fawn nestled closely with Sam under the belly of one of the horses. Their shelter was just big enough to block the blowing windstorm. They sat for two hours dozing off and on, till, just as suddenly as it had started, the wind stopped. There was an eerie silence all around them as they got to their feet.

They wiped all the animals' eyes with wet hands and gave each of them a drink. Sam looked at their surroundings and saw they could walk out of their shelter up a low sloping dune. The sky was beginning to turn to a clear blue in the southwest, where the windstorm had come from. In the northeast the blue was hidden by a huge swirling brown cloud.

When they reached the top of the dune they were only twenty yards from a small body of brown covered water.

A herd of about fifty horses stood on the other side of the small lake. The animals were hobbled in a circle around a cluster of sand covered humps on the ground. While Sam and Fawn watched, the mounds began moving and rising out of the desert floor.

The two made their way watchfully around the lake, keeping close to the water's edge. When they got a little closer they could see the group was Indians. Fawn recognized them as Utes, the same as Red Eagle's family.

"Mike-to-burn." Fawn greeted them before the Indians had even seen them approaching.

"Mike-to-burn." The startled elder returned her welcome.

Fawn talked to the old man, and his squaw who seemed to be the one in charge. Sam stood silently watching as the three waved their arms about, pointing to the brown sky.

"Kawn-pi-equay," The old woman told Fawn they were going home to Ute Mountain.

Fawn held her hand out in Sam's direction and told the woman elder that he was her husband.

"Att-um-bar." The old man injected.

"Att-um-bar." Fawn responded "Good talk."

The talk was over. The Ute band simply and quietly mounted and followed the lake around, walking in Sam and Fawn's footsteps.

They watched the Utes follow the dark cloud to the east then mounted their ponies and rode toward the snow topped mountains.

"Not very friendly." Sam commented. "Not like Red Eagle."

"They in hurry to get to Manitou" Fawn answered. The Utes had not yet found the true God.

It took them another three days of uneasy riding to follow the river out of the ever moving, shifting dunes. Their eyes were vigilant to the southwest, looking for another sand storm.

With the San Juan Mountains as a backdrop Sam and Fawn were quietly excited to see the evergreens spring up along the river and in the surrounding countryside. Fall colors brightly displayed the reds, yellows, and oranges of God's Glory as they entered the last leg of their journey. Quaking aspens shimmered in the breeze, appearing as gold coins, sparkling in the sunshine.

It was the most beautiful sight either of them had ever seen. Sometime in the next week they would begin looking for their home place.

———————— ….. ————————

The river forked and on the south fork they came into an opening that housed a multitude of activity. Large corrals and barns held several teams of horses and a few mule teams.

In front of the main corral was a stagecoach way station. There were eight small rooms occupying the upper floor for overnights stops. A large gathering room down stairs held a huge fireplace and cook- fire combination. A long table with benches on each side served as a feeding trough for mostly coarse characters with very few table manners.

Sam and Fawn were not too keen on being around a bunch of rowdies but Sam thought it would be good for Fawn to have a warm place and a better meal than the trail food they had been eating. As they rode into the yard a loud cry to a team of horses sent a mud wagon on its way. These were smaller lighter open sided stagecoaches designed for rough mountainous terrain. They were called celerity wagons or mud wagons for the way they traversed some of the muddy rutted, mountain roads.

It was approaching dusk as the two arrived. The overnight passengers were just being seated at the table as Sam and Fawn slowly entered the big open room.

A scraggly stoop shouldered old man, wearing an apron and holding a large pot of beans greeted them.

"You want to eat, have a seat. You men scoot down and let these two sit."

As he passed a shelf on his way to the table the cook grabbed two porcelain plates and dropped them on the table.

"Cups are by the fire close to the coffee pot. Help yourself." He did not look up to see who came in.

As Sam threw his leg across the bench to sit, he heard someone say.

"Howdy, Mister Raines, see you made it to the Colorado Territory."

Startled, Sam looked up into the face of Kit Carson.

"Well I'll be. Good to see you Mister Carson. I thought you were still chasing Comancheros."

"No… Son…. I gave up the army. Going to do some ranching somewhere about here."

Two of the scruffy looking men at the other end of the table exchanged glances. The third one with them shook his head side to side, shushing the other two.

Kit Carson spoke to Sam again. "This is Mister Tobin, a friend of mine."

"How do Mister Raines. I'm Thomas Tate Tobin. How do Mam." He greeted Fawn.

Fawn quietly moved her head up and then looked at Sam.

"This is my wife Spotted Fawn. I think you remember Fawn, Mister Carson, she got away from them Comancheros." Sam reminded Kit Carson of the episode in New Mexico Territory.

One of the three men at the end of the table jumped to his feet. "You got a problem with Comanchers mister?" His hand fell to the revolver on his hip and he looked directly at Sam.

Sam, Kit Carson and Thomas Tobin were all surprised by the action. The man stepped away from the table and wrapped his hand around the six gun to pull it from the holster. Thomas Tobin shot him in the chest before he cleared leather and with a startled look he fell to the wooden floor.

"You other two looking for trouble too?" Last time I fooled with hombres like you I cut their heads off and put em in a sack. You want some of me?" Tobin's eyes took on a steely gray look.

The two owl hoots got up and started for the door. The old man with the apron on shouted. "Take your garbage with you. I ain't picking up your garbage."

One of the two reached for the Henry rifle the dead man had leaned against the bench.

"Leave it!" Kit Carson spoke this time.

The two men picked up the body and dragged it through the door. Horses thundered away from the station. The dead man lay on the ground outside by the hitching rail.

Another older clean cut man came through the door.

"Looks like I missed something," he quipped.

"Hello Charley." Kit Carson addressed the man.

"Howdy Kit, Thomas," He looked at Sam.

"Charley Reynolds, don't believe I know you folks."

"Sam Raines, Charley. This is his wife Spot... Uh, Fawn." Kit Carson introduced them. "Charley owns a small ranch at the Rio Grande headwaters. He wife is Ute. How long you married now, Charley?"

"Twenty years I reckon." Charley Reynolds smiled.

Fawn looked up at Charley then at Sam. A big smile came across her face.

"You gonna eat some of these beans Charley, or you want a steak. Might be one of your steers, but they ain't to tough." The stage wrangler laughed as he spoke to Charley Reynolds. Apparently they knew each other.

Charley Reynolds sat and they all had a steak, beans and biscuits. All of them but Fawn enjoyed a hot cup of coffee. She sat quietly as the men talked.

Charley had ridden in from Denver where he was looking for someone to bring him two hundred more head of longhorns brought up from Texas on the Santa Fe Trail. "I saw them two owl hoots in Denver. Seems they're following me. Don't know why. I spent all I had on beef cattle before I left Denver.

Charley was the first to leave. "Going to head for the ranch, I like my bed under the stars. I'm going to ride up the river a ways. Good moon out. Y'all take care."

SIXTEEN

There is an appointed time for everything .And there is a time for every event under heaven --- A time to give birth and a time to die. A time to plant and a time to uproot what is planted.
Ecclesiastes 3; 1-2

Sam and Fawn visited with Kit and Thomas Tobin for a short time. Kit asked them about their trip through the Rio Grande gorge.

When Sam told of losing their horses, all their supplies, and his Sharps rifle, Thomas Tobin pointed to the weapon that was left by the two comancheros.

"That looks like a Henry forty-four. I don't think he's gonna need it anymore. If his horse is still outside, there might be some cartridges in the saddle bags,"

The three men walked out into the moonlit night. Fawn trailed along behind, sticking close to Sam.

The way-station wrangler, who was also the cook, dragged the dead body, left by his cohorts, over to the river and kicked it into the flowing stream, grumbling to himself. As he walked by the horse tied to the rail he opened the saddlebag and threw a box of forty fours to Sam.

"I'll keep the horse, might be worth six bits to another one of that bunch.

"Where you headed Sam? Kit Carson asked.

"Up the river hadn't seen the start of the Rio Grande yet. That's what I came for, maybe do some beaver trapping. Sam contemplated his future with a new wife and a papoose on the way. He wanted to get somewhere and build them a shelter from the coming cold.

"Trapping beaver is about played out in the San Juan's. There are three things working up there right now. You cut timber, hunt for gold, or chase cows. Course, you can do all three if you really want to dig in and stay up there." Thomas Tobin laid it out for Sam.

"Afraid he's right, Sam" Kit threw in. "We're gonna do some ranching somewhere around here, maybe over by Crede."

Sam was not interested in following the two men to look for a ranch. He was still the loner. The episode earlier had reinforced his felling about people. He was happy for it to be just him and Fawn and wherever the Good Lord led them. It was in His hands.

The friends finally said their goodbyes. The husband and wife walked away up the river, leading their ponies. They stopped just out of sight of the stage relay station and curled up in their buffalo robes. There was no need for a fire. Their bellies, full of steak and beans would warm them from the inside out.

At first light, they mounted and began another day, another day nearer their destination. Sam rode with the Henry rifle across his legs with one hand on the trigger. He liked the Henry. It had a better feel than the Sharps and was easier to load than the bolt- action Sharps he had carried since the war.

The fall colors and the ever increasing number of spruce and pinion pine trees provided a canopy as they rode along the river bank. The shimmering aspen were a sight to behold.

In the afternoon they were drawing near to a place Kit Carson had described to them as wagon- wheel gap.

It was a gap with a natural flat alongside the river. It was a good place to take a rest and water the animals.

They rounded a bend onto the flat that had one lone spruce tree back away from the river bank. Fawn suddenly pulled back on her reins and pointed to the tree. Sam looked at the tree and back to Fawn. Lifting the Henry he shrugged his shoulders. Fawn pointed again. When Sam looked again he saw what she was pointing to.

A man laid face down in the grass with one hand up and an arm around the tree trunk. He was trying to pull himself up. Sam quickly kicked his horse forward. He galloped to the tree and slid down off the bare back of his big bay. Fawn followed close behind him.

When Sam got to the man he gently turned him over and leaned him against the tree.

"Shot....Shot in the back....Robbed." The man passed out.

Sam recognized him from the night before. It was Charley Reynolds, the rancher with a Ute wife, on his way home.

Fawn brought a canteen and helped Sam pour cool water over Charley's lips.

Charley opened his eyes once more. "Them two from last night. Tobin should have shot them all. They followed me from Denver. Didn't get anything."

"We got to get him patched up. He's losing lots of blood." Sam felt behind the ranchers back and found an entry wound. It was on his lower right side. "I think it went through. Let's get his vest and shirt off.

Between the two of them they managed to remove his shirt and vest. Fawn looked at the wound and got quickly to her feet. She made a mud pack at the river's edge, then searched around and pulled several green plants. Mixing the herbs with the mud she made a poultice like Sam had found on his shoulder once in a Texas cave .Tearing the sleeves from his shirt, Sam covered the mud healing poultice.

Fawn retrieved one of the buffalo robes and they wrapped Charley in it.

Fawn sat on the ground next to the wounded man while Sam looked around for tracks. The two robbers had crossed the river and high- tailed it away from and down the river.

The lessons taught the young Indian woman by her mother began to fill her mind. She built a fire and started a pot of water boiling. Into the pot she dropped buffalo jerky and smoked rabbit given to them by Red Eagles Ute Family. She scowered the riverside and pulled healing herbs to put in the boiling soup.

While Fawn prepared the herbal concoction, Sam looked around again for Charley's horse. When he checked the river once more he saw three sets of tracks. The robbers were also horse thieves.

He began cutting long green limbs and he and his wife constructed a travois.

"Sam," Charley Reynolds called his name. "Sam… must get home Blue Sparrow take care of me."

"We'll get you home, Charley. You sleep now. Spotted Fawn will take care of you till we get you there." Sam spoke quietly to the injured man.

When the broth had all boiled down to a thick liquid, Fawn woke the man and fed him the potion slowly. Sam remembered again, after a snake bite and broken leg, that Fawn had spooned a soup such as this into his mouth.

Sam felt Fawn get up twice during the night and watched   as she fed Charley the healing brew.

None of the three rested well, Charley probably had the best night's sleep. The herbs were meant to cause sleep and healing.

——————— ..... ———————

It was late October and the days were becoming colder. Dark gray and black ominous clouds swept over the San Juan Mountains dropping a blanket of snow at the higher elevations.

Charley was more coherent now when he woke. It had been three days since the two new friends had found him and saved his life. He rested well with the healing, sleep inducing herbs Fawn had forced into his system.

While he slept he dreamed about Blue Sparrow at the ranch without him. The cattle had to be brought down from the high country feeding grounds. His hands had long since cut the hay fields and bundled it for winter feed, they all knew what to do and would herd the cattle without him. All their ranch hands were Ute Indians, most of them his wife's family. He knew she would be cared for but also knew she was expecting him.

Slowly and meticulously they followed the winding Rio Grande from one pass to another.

Charley was getting restless on the travois and wanted to mount the pack horse that trudged along pulling him behind. Fawn would not allow it.

"You get home. You ride horse. Not now! Here …Read Bible while you ride." Fawn pushed her and Sam's New Testament into his hand. He rested and read the rest of the way.

Ten days after leaving- wagon wheel gap, they rounded a turn through a mountain pass. Charley recognized where he was.

"Whoa!" He shouted! "Whoa!" He began trying to climb out of the travois.

Sam dismounted and went back to help him to his feet.

"We're home!" He waved his arms around. "See those high cliffs over there? They run out of the ranch and into the Rio Grande Headwaters. See that water falling? See that long blue pool of beautiful water? That is it my friend. That's what you came eighteen hundred miles to see…. That is home." A tear formed in the corner of Charley Reynolds' eyes.

Sam turned and looked up the mighty Rio Grande. What a wonderful peaceful place it had turned into. He wrapped his arm around Fawn and they stood in awe of what was before them.

Charley was the next to speak. "That, my friends, is your Garden of Eden. I know your God too." He cut the travois loose and began to untie the buffalo robe from it. "I will walk from here. Will you join me?"

Blue Sparrow was standing on the front porch of a small log ranch house; her right hand shaded her eyes from the sun. There was smoke billowing out of a tall stone chimney in the room behind her. She saw a movement between the river and Reagan Lake, which was part of their ranch lands.

There were horses running free in the hay fields over that way, but these were grouped close and it appeared someone might be leading them.

An hour later she still watched the movement from the porch as it drew closer. She was finally able to make out the forms of three people. Who could they be? Charley would be alone and riding his horse, not walking as these people was doing.

She called to her brother "Pow-inch!" She had called him Beaver in his native tongue. "Get the rifle. We have company"

Blue Sparrow walked into the house and put a pot of coffee on the fire, then came right back out.

"None of those horses have saddles," She said to Beaver.

"Charley," he pointed to the three people walking toward them.

Blue Sparrow saw it at the same time Beaver did.

"Charley!" She yelled and jumped from the porch at a full run, "Charley!"

Charley Reynolds tried to run to his wife but the pain in his side would not allow him to.

To Charley it was good to be back home and safe in the care of Blue Sparrow, although he knew that Sam and Fawn had saved his life. He and Blue Sparrow were once young like Sam and Fawn. The only difference was they had never had children. That did not affect their love for each other.

Charley had come to the San Juan Mountains in eighteen forty five. Trapping the long cold winters in the mountains brought him into contact with the Utes. He had found Blue Sparrow and within a year they had settled on the Rocking 'R' Ranch.

The two mountain men and their brides talked late into the night that first day.

Sam and Fawn were shown to a room in the back corner of the log house. A fire had been started by one of Blue Sparrow's relatives. Sam had not slept in a bed since the great civil war. Fawn had never ever slept off the ground.

They sank down into the soft feather mattress. Fawn thought she was going to fall into a deep hole and be covered over and smothered by the mattress. They slept very little and were up and out before the sun came up.

Sam put wood into the cook fire in the small kitchen while Fawn prepared the coffee pot. While the coffee boiled the two of them walked through the big room and out onto the front porch. To their surprise, while they slept, God had covered the entire countryside with a thick white blanket.

This is where they wanted to be. They were home. Today Sam would ride the river looking for a place to build a cabin for his wife and child.

Charley and Blue Sparrow joined their guests on the porch. They, too, were glad to see the snow covered landscape.

"Sam.... I know you want a place of your own... But let me throw something out for you. Blue Sparrow and me talked after you went to bed..." He hesitated, "Sam we're getting old and are tired of chasing cows all over the mountain... After that gunshot... We need someone to help us. Someone like you... Someone, young."

"I don't know Mister Reynolds. I... We don't like to be around people." Sam still had the mind of a trapper.

"Look Sam... I owe you. I need help and I owe you. You want to be away from people. I'll have the ranch hands build you a cabin away from the house. We'll ride out and find a spot on the ranch. Stay till spring; trap a little if you want. The snows will get heavy soon. Think about it."

Charley saw a way to give back some of what the Lord had given them. Blue Sparrow, like Fawn had learned to read and spent much of her time in the Word.

Fawn had stood by quietly massaging the baby who was protruding in her belly and listening to her husband and Charley talk.

"Sam," She turned to Sam. "We stay till flower blooms, not on soft bed but we stay."

Sam looked to the clear, blue sky over the San Juan Mountains. A small, quiet voice spoke to his heart. You are home.

Sam suddenly knew that the Lord had brought him to this time and this place. "Forgive me Lord for being selfish. You have truly brought us home."

The following morning Sam and Charley rode across the river and found a place with a view of the beautiful blue pond that began the Rio Grande River.

---------- ….. ----------

Sam and Fawn spent much of that first cold winter watching the wildlife and trapping beaver down the river from the small homey cabin that their friends had provided for them. They did spend most of their time alone together, the way Sam wanted. He had been a wanderer since he had left home to go to war. After that horrible four years of turmoil he had been through, all he wanted was to be alone. Gradually, over the long snowy winter he became of the mind that it was good to be in a family again. He began to want to be with his wife and the dear friends who had offered to take them in and allow them to find their way.

They did not have a feather bed. Their bed in the cabin was a board deck covered with the buffalo robes given to them by Red Eagle's Ute family. Every morning it gave Fawn pleasure to make her man a pot of coffee in the same old blue porcelain pot she had used on the trail.

They had chosen to one day a week sleep under God's heavenly sky. They chose Tuesdays to sleep out under the stars, because Monday was the first day after the Sabbath and the start of a new week. There was always something to be done at the ranch on that day.

On the second Tuesday in March, Sam and Fawn Raines were under another of God's star studded nights.

In the early morning hours of Wednesday, March thirteenth, just as the sun peeked over the San Juan Mountains, Fawn told her husband, "It is time." She walked away from him into a cluster of Pinion trees and in the traditional way of her people gave birth to a man child. Sam waited nervously on the bank of the Rio Grande River. When he heard the loud strong cry of a newborn, he jumped to his feet.

Fawn brought the Papoose to its father. Sam lifted his naked son to the early morning sky at arm's length. "Lord, I offer to you Samson Castile Raines. Do with him as you may.

When he bowed his head to thank his wife for what she had given him and to tell her how much he loved her, a beautiful small scarlet paintbrush lifted its head through the soft melting snow to tell the world it was springtime and a new day was dawning.

Francis Louis Guy Smith

Made in the USA
Charleston, SC
02 October 2011